Mail Order Marm

Book 24 in Brides of Beckham

Kirsten Osbourne

Chapter One

DORIS BUTLER HAD BEEN in Salmon, Oregon for just over a month, and the town was already a different place. She hadn't come to town with the intention of changing everything and everyone, but it had happened anyway.

She sat at the table with her two closest friends, who were like sisters to her already. Gretchen was to her left, and the schoolteacher, Miss Frederica Hughes, was to her right.

"I've been thinking about your situation, Gretchen," Doris began. "I think we need to send for a mail order husband for you. It's not the way things are normally done, of course, but I'm sure my brother Darryl would come. He can work with Harv at the mill."

"Darryl is your twin, right?" Gretchen asked. It wasn't easy keeping up with Doris's thirteen siblings.

"He is. He's a good man, and if he doesn't treat you right, I can box his ears."

Rica laughed. "I'm not sure if we need more of your demon horde living here in Salmon . . ."

Doris stuck her tongue out at Rica. "I know Gretchen needs a husband. If she's still living at her mother's house when the baby is born, I'm afraid it's going to be terrible for her."

Gretchen sighed heavily. "You're right about that. My mother will never forgive me for getting pregnant out of wedlock. It's not my fault my fiancé was lost at sea, but she sure seems to think so." She patted her belly. "We only have two months, though."

"I know . . . so here's my plan. I'm going to wire my sister and tell her to put Darryl on the first train out here. I'll make sure she knows that you're pregnant because even my brother doesn't deserve *that* kind of surprise. But when he gets here, you two can marry. I have to talk to Harv yet, but we all know that's just a formality. The man is practically working himself to death to fill all the orders he gets. He needs a helper."

Gretchen and Rica exchanged a look.

"I'm not so sure about this plan of yours, Doris . . ." Gretchen said with a frown. "Your brother deserves to be with someone who's not already huge with another man's baby."

Doris sighed. "We're talking about the brother who insisted I put newspaper on the barn floor *before we painted the cow purple.*"

"Still . . . He's been a good brother to you, which is why you're suggesting he marry me. Are you sure you want him tied to a woman who has a bad reputation?"

"Demon. Horde." Doris shook her head. "I promise you he's used to having a bad reputation, and he cares just about as much as I do. Let me telegraph Lizard Breath."

Gretchen bit her lip. "I don't know if I'm ready to marry someone. Reginald was the love of my life. How can I just ignore that and marry someone else?"

"It's your choice. But I think Reginald would want you to do it for the baby."

Rica nodded as well. "I think so, too, Gretchen."

Gretchen buried her face in her hands. "Fine. Do it." Her heart sank as she said the words, but she knew the women sitting with her, her two best friends, had only her best interests at heart. She'd do it, because she didn't know what else to do.

DARRYL MILLER STOOD in the field, wiping the sweat from his forehead with a bandana. He longed for a way to leave Beckham, Massachusetts and never return. Some of his sisters had become mail order brides, traveling to the west for adventures, but as a man, he couldn't do that.

He nodded to his father, pointing toward the house. He needed to go in and take a quick water break. They'd been at it since sun-up, and it was after five. Harvest season was always the busiest.

When he got to the house, he was surprised to see his sister Elizabeth there, quietly chatting with their mother. Elizabeth wasn't exactly a stranger, but she usually came out for holidays or invited one or two of her siblings to come and visit her at once. He couldn't remember the last time she'd just dropped in for a visit in the middle of the week.

"Hey, Lizard Breath." Darryl had never gotten out of the habit of calling her by her childhood nickname. He was pretty sure none of their siblings had either. It just felt good and familiar. Elizabeth lived in a mansion in town and ran a big business, so it felt good to bring her back down to their level.

Elizabeth just smiled at him, obviously not bothered. Their mother was snuggling Elizabeth's baby, happy to have a grandchild in her house for a while. "I'm actually here to see *you,* Darryl."

He blinked at her. "Me? Why? You have a bride out west that's looking for a groom to come marry her?"

"You think you're kidding . . . Doris has a friend. She's very pregnant. Her fiancé died at sea right before their wedding. She's been pretty much ostracized in the town. Doris's husband Harv would give you a job in the sawmill. They want you on the next train."

"Seriously? Why me?" Darryl had never dreamed of going off to be a mail order groom. Sure, their brother Wally had done it years before, but Wally had always been a bit odd.

"I'm not sure. Doris says that you're the man. I think she misses having her twin around." Elizabeth smiled at him. "Are you interested?"

Darryl sat down heavily, still trying to figure out if this was something he'd even think about being interested in. A marriage to a strange pregnant woman, who had been ostracized by her town. But his sister Doris, who had impeccable taste in friends, wanted him to marry her. And he'd have a non-farming job in the west. Oregon. Near the coast, from what he understood.

"I think I am. We should be done with harvest tomorrow night."

"Then you can leave on Tuesday? I'm going to go and wire Doris back. She's going to be so excited to get to see her favorite brother." Elizabeth got to her feet and reached down for her baby. "Come on, Benjamin. Let's go home."

"Did you walk?" Darryl asked.

"Sure. I may live in the city now, but I'm still the farmgirl who grew up in this house." Elizabeth had never put on airs, and she never would. Once a farmgirl, always a farmgirl.

"Let me hitch up the wagon and drive you back. I can't imagine walking that far with a baby in your arms."

Elizabeth laughed. "I won't say no to the ride, but I'm perfectly capable of walking."

"I don't think you're some hot house pansy now that you live in your big house, but I have a hard time believing you enjoy the thirty-minute walk while carrying my nephew." He stood up. "Wait here while I hitch up the wagon."

Ten minutes later, they were on their way. "What more do you know about this girl?" he asked as soon as they were out of earshot of their mother.

"Her name is Gretchen. She's kind and loving. No one speaks to her, and some of the ladies in town even tried to shun her!" Elizabeth shook her head. "All of this came from letters and not from the telegram. The telegram was bare-bones, asking specifically for you to marry Gretchen."

"What do I need to take with me? I've never even been on a train before." He was flummoxed and excited all at once.

"Everything you want. If there's something that won't reasonably fit into a couple of bags or a trunk, then I can ship whatever it is to you. I'm betting you won't marry the day you arrive because you won't have a place to live. Gretchen still lives with her parents, but she may have planned to have a house with Reginald that you could move into. Not sure about that part of things."

"Will Doris meet me at the train station?"

Elizabeth laughed. "I'm sure she will. I'll tell her that's a requirement of you coming. She'll probably have her twins, Pris and Pauline with her."

"I can't wait to meet them. And hug the stuffing out of Doris. It feels like it's been years since I've seen her."

"I think you two were closer to each other than any of the rest of us. Susan and I were always close, but it didn't bother me too much when she moved to Texas. It's always bothered you that Doris moved to Oregon."

Darryl shrugged, neither confirming nor denying his sister's words. "I miss her. We're supposed to be together."

"I think she feels the same, and that's why she asked for you specifically. I really am glad you're willing to go. Her friend Gretchen sounds like a very nice girl, and since she's had a baby on the way, her mother has been very difficult to live with. I almost feel like you're riding in there as a knight in shining armor to rescue her."

"How about a farmer in a plaid shirt?" he asked.

Elizabeth laughed as he pulled up in front of her house. She kissed his cheek. "Thanks for the ride, little brother. Come to town tomorrow night and spend the night in one of our spare rooms. Then we'll send you off Wednesday morning. I'm going to send Bernard to the telegraph office."

"You mean he's home, and he didn't bother to drive you? I always thought he was a better man than that." Darryl shook his head.

"I told him I wanted to walk and I'd get a ride back with one of my brothers." Elizabeth grinned at him as she climbed down, the baby in her arms. "See you tomorrow!"

Darryl was laughing as he drove off. His sister really was an independent woman. He couldn't even express how proud he was of her.

WHEN DARRYL'S TRAIN started to get close to Salmon, Oregon, his nerves got the better of him. He thought about getting off the train at the stop before Salmon, just because he wasn't sure if he could get off and marry a total stranger. What had he agreed to?

He closed his eyes and prayed that not only would his sister be at the train station waiting for him, but that his new bride would be excited to see him. He was worried about her still being in love with the man she'd been engaged to . . . the father of her child. He wondered if he'd be able to think of himself as the child's father quickly. He hoped so, for all of their sakes.

When the conductor called out his stop, "Salmon, Oregon!" he got to his feet, breathing deeply. Looking out the window, he tried to spot his sister, but he couldn't see her through the seats and people in them.

Stepping off onto the platform, he looked around, trying to spot Doris and his new bride. Instead, he was engulfed in a hug by arms that he'd always considered scrawny. "Doris!"

"Darryl, I have to admit I've missed you. It's so good to have you here!" Doris stepped back and introduced him to her twin daughters. "Pris, this is your uncle Darryl. Pauline, meet your uncle." She smiled at Darryl. "If you have trouble telling them apart, Pris has green eyes and Pauline has blue. They're almost identical otherwise until you get to know them."

"I'm glad it was easier to tell us apart than that . . . just look down the front of the diaper." Darryl winked at her, and she laughed.

"You're a mess."

"I am." He looked around. "Where's my bride?"

Doris frowned. "I'm really not sure. She was supposed to be at my house thirty minutes ago, so we could walk over together. I waited until the last minute. Hopefully she'll be there when we arrive."

"Could something have happened to her?"

"I really don't know. Her mother isn't exactly fond of her, but I don't think she'd sit back and let her be injured in any way." Doris shrugged. "I'm sure she'll be waiting for us. I didn't lock the house, so she could just go in. She may not have felt up to the walk today either. She's pretty close to her time."

Darryl picked up both of his bags and walked alongside his sister. "Nice little town."

"It really is. Well, it's getting nicer, we'll say. It's growing fast, and all of the lumber goes through Harv's sawmill. He's really glad he's going to have someone to work beside him."

"It's nice of you to have a job ready for me when you sent for me. I'm excited to be in the west and not be farming anymore. I swear if I had to pick one more bug off a plant, I would have screamed." Darryl shook his head. No one knew his hatred of farming quite like Doris did.

"I understand completely." She stopped in front of a building. "This is the sawmill. Our house is out back. Let me introduce you to Harv, and then hopefully we'll go to my house and find Gretchen waiting for you."

Harv shut off the saw and walked over to them. "This is your twin? Darryl, right?" He offered his hand to shake.

"Yes, it's good to meet you. From Doris's letters home, it's obvious she thinks a lot of you," Darryl responded, gripping his new brother-in-law's hand. "Thanks for the job offer. I won't let you down."

"If you're anything like your sister, you'll exceed every expectation I don't know I have yet."

Darryl laughed. "Doris is pretty exceptional."

Harv smiled. "I hope you're ready to work first thing in the morning. I'm going to finish up for the night, but I have orders coming out my ears. I need a man working beside me, and I can't wait."

"I can start now! Just give me a minute to get changed into work clothes."

Harv looked at Doris, obviously hoping that she would consent. "Yes?"

"No," Doris said, shaking her head. "He's been on a train for days. Asking him to start tomorrow is too soon in my opinion, but I understand how behind you are. And I know how hard my brother is used to working. He's not going to want to wait to get started."

Darryl shrugged. "I guess I'm starting tomorrow. I promise you will get what you pay for, having a Miller on your payroll."

"No doubt in my mind." Harv waved as his wife, daughters, and brother-in-law headed around the sawmill to his home.

Doris opened the door, fully expecting to see Gretchen sitting at the table waiting for her. Instead, her two older boys, and her other close friend, Rica were waiting, along with a note addressed to Doris. Rica was the boys' teacher, and she often went home with them after school to visit their mother and Gretchen.

"What's the note?" Doris asked, reaching for it.

"No idea," Rica answered. "I just got here, so I helped myself to tea and cookies. I knew you'd be here soon. I had to meet this practically perfect brother of yours." She stood up and offered her hand to shake. "I'm Rica, the local schoolteacher."

"That's an unusual name," Darryl said, smiling at the woman. He'd never met a schoolteacher he was fond of, but this one had pretty golden curls coming out of her bun, and he wanted to remove each pin and see what happened when her hair flowed free.

Rica was aware that Doris was reading the note, so she continued to try to occupy her friend's brother. "It's really Frederica, but that's such a mouthful. My father started calling me Rica before I could walk."

"I like it." Darryl looked at his sister. "So? What's the deal?"

Doris sighed. "Gretchen couldn't go through with the marriage. She's not ready for anyone to replace Reginald in her life."

Darryl frowned. "What am I supposed to do now?"

Chapter Two

RICA LOOKED BACK AND forth between brother and sister. "I'll marry you." She hadn't meant for the words to pop out of her mouth, but they had. She immediately wanted to crawl under the table, but she couldn't show cowardice. Two of her pupils were in the very next room!

Darryl and Doris both looked at her as if she'd lost her mind. "Really?" Doris asked. "I was planning on talking you into a mail order groom after Gretchen was settled."

Darryl frowned at his sister. "Just because you're happily married doesn't mean the whole world needs to be." He concentrated his attention on Rica. "Maybe we should talk for a moment. Decide if this is what we want to do." He knew he wanted to make sure they had chemistry between them before they made any rash decisions.

Rica didn't want to talk about it. She wanted to do something impulsive for the first time in her life and go to Pastor Savoy and get married. Why not? If Gretchen could do it with a baby on the way, she could do it when she didn't have another person to worry about. She'd never even kissed a man, but she was sure her lips wouldn't fall off or anything.

Finally, she nodded. "Let's go for a walk, and we can talk." Thankfully it was Friday afternoon, and her parents weren't expecting her that weekend. In the past month, she'd spent more weekends in Salmon than ever before. Having friends had changed the town for her.

Darryl smiled at his sister and opened the door for Rica. He wasn't sure what to say. He found her very attractive, but . . . she was a schoolteacher. He was more apt to put a toad in a schoolteacher's lunch pail than he was to marry one.

Rica automatically walked away from the center of town. She didn't want people to see them and assume they were courting, just to find out that they weren't going to marry after all.

They'd walked over a minute without either of them saying a word, so Darryl cleared his throat. "Tell me about you. Are you from here?"

"I'm from the next town over. This is my second year to teach here in Salmon. Before this, I taught in the school I went to growing up. This school offered a little more money, but more importantly, it offered me independence. Your sister's kids almost ran me off, and from what I understand, they've run the past three teachers off."

He chuckled. "The Butler brats. We've been called the demon horde for so long, I really understand where the boys are coming from."

Rica sighed. "They've been much better behaved this year. I find I'm very impressed with how your sister handles them."

"I think those of us that were . . . precocious children tend to make better parents." They kept walking until they were outside of town, and he turned to her. "I think I'm willing to give it a try between us, but I need to know one thing first."

She sucked in a breath, surprised. She'd always been a schoolmarm, and she had never expected a man to show any interest in her. Especially a man who was so handsome. "What's that?"

"I need to know if there's magic between us."

"Magic?" she asked, frowning at him. "What do you mean?"

"I mean I want to kiss you and see if there's any chemistry." He reached out and put his hands on her shoulders, pulling her toward him. "May I kiss you, Rica?" With as close as they stood, he marveled at how thick her eyelashes were. She wore spectacles, and they seemed to magnify her eyes a bit. He wanted to pluck them off her face and see what she looked like without them.

Rica looked up and down the road both ways, and then nodded. She couldn't risk being seen kissing a man she'd met minutes before by any of the parents of the children she taught. She could lose her job.

He slowly lowered his head, pressing his lips to hers. As soon as their mouths touched, he felt as if an electric current was flowing through his body. He gathered her closer, deepening the kiss. After a moment, he had his answer, and he stepped back. He was out of breath, and her glasses were slightly fogged up.

Right there, on the dirt road leading out of Salmon, Oregon, he got down on one knee. "I don't have a ring to give you, but that doesn't make the sentiment any less real. Will you be my wife, Rica whatever-your-last-name-is?"

Rica felt a hysterical laugh bubbling up inside her. Never in her entire twenty-five years had she done anything impulsive. Not one thing. And here she was standing on the side of the road, looking down at a man she'd just kissed after mere minutes' acquaintance. "Why yes, Darryl, whose last name I really do know. I'll marry you."

He got to his feet, taking her hand and pulling her toward him, kissing her again. "Let's go find the preacher."

"You don't even want to know where we'll live?" She couldn't believe he was ready to marry her so quickly. Weren't there details to work out?

He frowned. "Are you boarding with someone here in town? I hadn't thought about that. We probably should have a home . . ."

She laughed. "I live in the teacherage behind the school. It's small, but it's certainly adequate for a newly married couple."

"Oh, good. Let's go get my sister and get married. I'm done dilly-dallying. I have to work in the morning." He pulled her back toward town. "You don't mind if my sister is there? And my nieces and nephews?"

"Not at all. Your sister has become one of my very closest friends. It's like our souls knew each other the very instant we met."

"You know, I've always felt that way about her too. Of course . . . we are twins . . ."

She grinned at that. He was as light-hearted as she was serious … or so it seemed. She needed someone with a sense of humor to balance her out. Maybe she wouldn't spend every waking moment thinking about teaching. Having a real life would be very nice.

"After we get your sister and the kids, we'll walk to Pastor Savoy's house. His wife is … painful at times, but he's a nice man. I don't think his wife has talked to your sister since she got here without saying at least once that she's praying for her with those children of hers."

He sighed. "Yup, sounds like they have the exact same reputation we always had. I hope Doris ignores her."

"I'm actually very impressed with your sister. I don't know if you know what's happened in this town since she arrived, but there was an older woman—Mrs. Lindon—who completely controlled *all* of the women in town. She told the other women that they were shunning Gretchen as a group, and as a result, no one would speak to her until your sister got here. Mrs. Lindon had everyone shun Doris when she refused to stop speaking to Gretchen. And then they all shunned me because I was friends with both of them."

"I don't see Doris taking any of that sitting down. We weren't raised with a lot of discipline, but we were raised to think for ourselves." Darryl could just imagine what Doris would do in that situation.

"She rallied all of the woman. It was a full-scale coup against Mrs. Lindon's leadership. I don't think she was looking to have all of the women come to her for advice, but that's what she's got now. She's completely taken Mrs. Lindon's place in this little town." Rica loved relating the story. She was so proud of her friend, it was ridiculous.

"Sounds like my sister. She's a pretty incredible person." He opened the door of his sister's house to let her precede him inside. Doris was cooking, and a pregnant woman he'd not yet met was sitting at her table. He couldn't help but wonder if this was the missing Gretchen.

The woman got to her feet. "I'm so sorry, Darryl. I hope you'll forgive me."

Darryl nodded, smiling. It was definitely Gretchen. "I will forgive you with no problem. I'm marrying Rica."

Gretchen laughed. "Well, I guess that worked out then. I just . . . I can't marry before Reginald's baby is even born. I'd feel like I was being disrespectful to his memory. I'm afraid I'm still in love with him."

"I understand that completely. I don't know if I could have been married to you without worrying about what he would have thought and felt. It feels like he's too important to your life for you to give up just now."

She sighed in relief. "I'm so glad you understand." Turning to Rica, she hugged her friend. "And I'm excited you're getting married! May I come to the wedding?"

Rica smiled. "How could I get married without my Salmon sisters?"

"I don't know if I can get married with three fishy-smelling women in the vicinity, but I'll do my best . . ." Darryl said, a grin on his face.

Doris wrinkled her nose at him. "We're at the point in the supper-making process where I can be gone for exactly an hour. Let's go get this wedding done!"

"I feel like you're pressuring me to do it fast," Darryl said, wrapping his arm around his twin and hugging her tight.

"Yup. That's exactly what's happening." Doris called for the children, and the eight of them set off down the street for the pastor's house. "We look like we're setting out to cause some sort of mayhem."

"Well, we're two of the demon horde and four Butler brats. Between the six of us, we could make some pretty crazy things happen, I think." Darryl's mind automatically went to mischief making, but he tried to tamp it down. There was no need to cause trouble, though it was always a bit fun.

One of the boys—and he didn't know which was which yet—turned to him and frowned. "We don't like being called the Butler brats. We're very well-behaved now, right, Miss Hughes?"

Rica nodded. "Oh definitely. You're like two totally different boys than you were at this time last year. I'm very proud of the progress you've made."

Both boys seemed to walk a little taller, and Darryl smiled. "Since you're my nephews, I could have taught you some fun new tricks, but I'm marrying the schoolmarm, so I have to be loyal to her first."

The older boy—he really needed to learn their names—turned to him and grinned. "Maybe you can tell us stories about what you and Ma did. We'd be very amused and promise not to mimic you. I don't think a joke is as good if you don't think of it yourself anyway."

Rica gave Darryl her best schoolteacher look. "I don't think that's a very good idea." The boys had been well-behaved, but getting new ideas was not something she wanted for them.

Darryl sighed. "I have to listen to my wife. What if she makes me stand in the corner all night at home?"

Both boys giggled. "I had to stand in the corner a lot last year," the younger boy said. "And we're still not allowed to go into the mercantile. We apologized and helped clean up the mess, but I don't think Mrs. Gottweiler is ever going to forgive us. *Ever!*"

"Sometimes saying you're sorry just isn't enough. Even if you do help pick up the mess."

"Like when you and Ma painted the cow purple?" the older boy said to him.

Darryl laughed. "She told you about that, did she? I think that's the day our sister Lizard Breath started planning how she was going to get out of the house and away from us. Two years later, she was living in the biggest house you ever saw, and she was sending women off to marry strangers. She did a lot to get away from your Ma and me."

Doris grinned at him. His words were true, though certainly not the entire story. "Well, soon we'll both be married, and the wonderful people of Beckham, Massachusetts will be able to tell stories about us forever."

"Our memories will live on in infamy!" Darryl grinned over at Rica, who was trying not to laugh. "Do you want to join me in my infamy?"

"I'm not sure about that . . . I like teaching a lot, and if I join you in your infamy, I might end up jobless." Rica grinned at him. She really did like his devil-may-care attitude about everything. It was very endearing. "This is the pastor's house." Rica drew a deep breath, suddenly nervous about the ceremony . . . and what would come after.

They walked to the house, and he knocked on the door. When a woman opened it, she frowned at them. Her eyes caught Doris's, and she said, "I'm still praying for you."

Doris smiled sweetly. "This is my brother, Darryl, and he's here to marry our own schoolteacher, Rica. Would your husband be available to perform the wedding?"

Mrs. Savoy shook her head. "I hope he plans to help you with your hellions . . ." She opened the door wide. "Come in."

"I brought my hellions with me. I'll try not to let them destroy your parlor while we wait." Doris had each of the twins' hands, and the boys had their hands behind their backs.

Mrs. Savoy rushed from the room. "Melvin! Hurry before our entire house is destroyed!"

Gretchen looked at Doris and giggled. "That was rather mean of you to play off her fears that way."

"Sometimes being nice just hurts too much!" Doris sat down on one of the sofas, holding the twins on her lap. The boys were on either side of her, looking perfectly innocent. Of course, they all knew that the innocent look was sure to send the pastor's wife into a fit of apoplexy.

Pastor Savoy walked into the room, a smile on his face. "You sure do have my wife running scared of your children, Mrs. Butler. I approve!"

Doris grinned. "My brother, Darryl, wants to marry Frederica Hughes, the local schoolteacher. I believe I introduced you at church last Sunday." Rica had been going home to her parents' house every weekend, and only in the past month had she gone to the local church and met some more of the people in the town she worked in.

"Ah, yes, of course. It's nice to see you again, Miss Hughes." The pastor picked up his Bible. "Let's get this wedding going."

Darryl and Rica took their places in front of the pastor, and he took her hand in his, offering what comfort he could. He could feel her nervousness, and he didn't want to add to it.

Ten minutes later, they were pronounced husband and wife. "Go ahead and kiss your bride, son." The pastor grinned. He was a jovial man, and Darryl liked him instantly. He was sure he wouldn't be preaching hellfire and brimstone like the pastor back in Beckham.

Darryl reached out for Rica and pulled her to him, kissing her softly. "Happy wedding day, wife."

Rica stood there staring at him, and suddenly the most important thing in her mind was trying to remember if she'd made her bed that morning. She was usually neat and orderly at all times, but she'd slept a little later than she should have. *Oh, dear, I don't know if it's made or not!*

Darryl turned to the pastor and shook his hand. "Thank you, sir."

"You're very welcome. I hope to see you in church on Sunday."

"Oh, definitely. I never miss church." And he never had. There was no better place to pull pranks on unsuspecting people.

"Let's all head back to my place, and I'll feed us all a nice wedding supper. I could probably even manage to bake a cake," Doris said, getting to her feet.

"Chocolate?" Pris asked, her eyes dancing with excitement.

"Only if you and your sister can lick the bowl for me. You know that's the most important step . . ."

"We will!" Pauline said excitedly.

"That better mean we get to share the frosting," one of the boys said. Darryl promised himself he was going to learn the names of those boys before the day was over. He didn't care what it took. A man should know the names of all his nieces and nephews.

Taking his new wife's hand in his, he led the way out of the pastor's house and back down the street. He was married. He didn't feel any different, but every time he glanced at is beautiful wife, his heart beat just a little bit faster.

Chapter Three

RICA FELT ODDLY AS she walked hand-in-hand with her new husband toward her friend's house. For a moment, she worried one of her students or their parents would see her, but it didn't matter anymore. She was a married woman. There was nothing in the town's charter about a schoolteacher marrying during her term, so unlike being seen in an ice cream parlor, this couldn't be used against her.

Darryl was joking around with the others and making the boys laugh. She felt a bit distanced from it all. He was obviously a man who enjoyed being the center of attention, while she tended to be more of a wallflower. She certainly hoped it was true what people said about opposites attracting, because she desperately wanted her marriage to work.

She was glad she wasn't going home to Pennington over the weekend because she wasn't sure how she could explain to her parents that she'd married a stranger. Hopefully by the time she'd been married for a week, she'd have a good explanation in place, and her parents would accept it.

Rica dove into helping with supper as soon as they were back at Doris's house. Gretchen took a seat and picked up the sewing project she'd been working on. So much sewing had needed to be done when Doris arrived that Gretchen had immediately begun helping.

The cake was in the oven and the frosting was whipped up by the time Harv walked in the door from work. He walked straight to his wife and kissed her softly. He smiled at Gretchen. "Best wishes."

Gretchen shook her head. "Rica married him."

Harv looked very confused for a moment, and he looked at his brother-in-law with surprise. "Now how did that happen?"

Darryl shrugged. "Gretchen didn't want to marry anyone but the father of her baby. Rica said she'd marry me, and I think she's awfully pretty, so I figured why not? I came here to marry a stranger, and that's just what I did."

Rica turned from the bread she was slicing. "He did ask me properly on one knee, though."

"He did?" Doris asked. "Why didn't I get to see this? Don't you know how much I would have loved to see Darryl on one knee? Did you make him grovel?"

Darryl stuck his tongue out at his sister. He hadn't realized just how childish she made him feel until that very moment. "She was very good about it, even though I couldn't remember her last name."

"What do last names matter? She was about to change hers to Miller anyway. The kids are going to have fun learning to call you Mrs. Miller, aren't they?" Harv asked.

Bobby hurried into the kitchen then, a confused look on his face. Bobby was the older of the two Butler boys, and he usually spoke for both of them. "Are we supposed to call you Aunt Rica now? Or do we call you Mrs. Miller? Or do we still call you Miss Hughes? Things are getting really confusing around here!"

Rica laughed. "You'll call me Aunt Rica at home and Mrs. Miller at school. Will that work for you?"

Bobby shook his head. "It's going to be awfully hard to remember, but I'll do my best."

"That's all I've ever asked of you, isn't it?" Rica asked as he headed back out of the room to tell his brother the answer to the question. Her eyes met Darryl's. "You're causing much confusion among the pupils of Salmon."

"Not deliberately!" Darryl protested. "I guess you could bring me to school for show and tell, so they can see why your name changed."

Harv shook his head at that. "Most certainly not. I'm going to keep you so busy at the sawmill, you'll forget you have a wife from seven in the morning 'til six at night. Monday through Saturday."

Rica frowned at that. "You're not even getting tomorrow off?" She had hoped they would have the entire weekend to get used to one another. It had to be strange enough to get used to living with a man you loved, but marrying a stranger? She definitely needed some time.

"I can't spare him. I'm sorry, Rica, you know I would if I could, but I've got orders piled up. I've promised everyone I'd have help starting tomorrow, so I will need to have him work starting tomorrow."

Darryl smiled at his wife. "It'll be nice to have the extra money coming in. You'll see." He could see she was disappointed.

Rica wasn't entirely sure about that. She wanted to spend the entire weekend getting to know her new husband before returning to work on Monday. "I guess we'll have to make the most of our Sundays off then." She wondered if he'd care for a picnic. She'd always thought picnics were terribly romantic, and though she'd never had a beau to fix a picnic for, she'd dreamed about it often. She'd pack a picnic before church on Sunday, and the two of them would have a lovely lunch somewhere private.

"Don't worry, Rica. I'll get him caught up, and then he'll let me have two days off per week. You'll see."

Harv shrugged. "I hope you can catch me up, but I have a feeling, it's going to be like this for a good long while."

Darryl shrugged. "I happen to like working, as long as I'm not farming, so I'm sure I'll enjoy every minute of it."

SHORTLY AFTER THEY finished supper and cake, Darryl got to his feet. "I appreciate the warm wishes and congratulations. Thanks for helping us make the most of our wedding day."

Rica smiled at him, glad he didn't mind getting up in front of groups and making little announcements like that. As much as she had to speak to her entire classroom full of children, everything changed when she had to talk to adults. "Are you ready to go?"

He nodded. "I'm more tired than I realized until just this moment. But spending that long on a train just makes you thankful when you put your feet on solid ground."

Doris frowned at Harv. "Are you sure you need him tomorrow? It really is an exhausting journey."

Harv sighed. "I wish I could give him the weekend off and let him start on Monday, but I really can't. It's important to our livelihood that he start working in the morning."

Darryl smiled at his brother-in-law. "I understand, and it really is all right. I'm tired, but it's nothing a good night's sleep won't take care of." He grabbed his bags from beside the front door. "Lead the way, my lovely wife!"

Rica blushed. "Thanks, Doris." She hugged her friend. "I'll probably stop by to talk tomorrow."

"I'd like that." Doris looked at Gretchen. "All three of us?"

"Like I would be anywhere else!" Gretchen said with a laugh.

Rica led the way out of the house, walking toward the school and teacherage. "I met your sister when I set up a meeting with her to talk about the behavior of her boys. She was more than willing to work with me on getting them on the right track, and we were friends before I left. It was amazing how well we just clicked. She and Gretchen and me. We were the outcasts." She knew he knew some of the story, and she was babbling more to cover the silence than anything. "I hate that it's getting dark so early."

"It's that time of year," he said. "I helped finish up the harvest in Beckham and then I left to come here. My dad needed me to do my share." It felt strange knowing they were going to her house to be alone. He'd never been quite that alone with a woman he wasn't related to.

"About tonight . . . we can wait a while to consummate if it makes you feel better. I'm all for doing it right away, but I can understand a woman not being as comfortable with that."

Rica thought about it for a moment. "Why don't we take a week to court and see what happens from there? I've never been courted, and I love the idea of it."

"I've never courted anyone. My family was pretty much ostracized in our area because of the demon horde thing. I know you already know about it, so I'm not going to get into it too much, but it was hard to find someone to court or to even let me talk to her at a barn dance."

"You went to barn dances?" she asked. She'd always wanted to do something like that.

"A few. But there was no dancing for me because all of the young ladies in the area knew to stay away from me." He sighed. "We'll figure this courting thing out together."

"Maybe we could do a dance in the school house next Friday night. To celebrate our wedding, or harvest, or the fact that we live in a free land." She didn't know why, but suddenly she felt like she needed to dance with him—to have that part of courting she'd always looked forward to but never had.

"In other words, you don't care what we call it, just so you get to go to a dance?"

"As long as you promise to dance with me. I've never actually gone to a dance because I was always afraid I'd end up being a wallflower, and no one would ever ask me to dance. I love to dance." Rica had practiced with her own brother for hours on end, but she'd never found the courage to actually go to one of the dances by herself. She'd prayed to be asked to the dance, but when she wasn't, she wasn't about to risk her feelings by standing alone.

He grinned. "I would love to dance with my beautiful wife. I'm surprised you even have to ask." He glanced at her sideways. "How much further?"

She pointed. "That's the schoolhouse up ahead, and the teacherage is right behind it. I hope you don't feel too cramped in it." She realized then she only had one bed in the little house. They would have to share it whether they were ready to be intimate or not. Why hadn't she thought of that sooner?

Darryl stopped in front of the school. "You should show me the schoolhouse. I want to see where my little wife disciplines students and turns them into thinking machines."

"I'm not sure about my students being thinking machines. In fact, I'm sure most of them aren't. They come to school because their parents make them. Most of them plan to be farmers, fishermen, farmer's wives, or fishermen's wives. There's never any variation. They know what kind of culture they come from, and they have no desire to rise above it."

"Does that make it hard to teach them?" He knew it had been similar at their little country school outside of Beckham. Everyone had known what they'd do from the moment they were born.

"It does sometimes. They don't understand why they need to know how to read and write when their jobs will likely have nothing to do with that. I convince the girls that they want to be able to read so they can follow recipes. The boys need math so they won't be cheated when they bring their catch into the market. That kind of thing. I wish I could get them to want knowledge just for the sake of knowledge, but that's not happening anytime soon." She opened the door to the schoolhouse and walked along the desks. "The school is big enough for twenty pupils. We have that many in the winter, but in the spring and fall, it's more like fifteen. The bigger boys stay home to help with the chores."

He nodded. "That's how it was back home, too. My sisters could do math in circles around me because I never got as much of an education as they did. My father said it was just the way of the world, and I needed to be happy I could go to school in the winter."

Rica sighed. "It seems to be the way of farming communities everywhere. Hopefully one day that will all change and school will be mandatory for children all nine months of the year."

He stopped and looked at her desk. "If I were your student, I'd have spent a lot of time in the corner."

"I'm sure you would. Or getting your knuckles rapped with a ruler."

"Do you do that?" he asked. All of his teachers had believed in rapping the knuckles of the most undisciplined of their pupils, and that was usually him and his siblings. His parents had never believed in corporal punishment, but they'd never argued when the teachers had meted it out.

She shrugged. "I never have. I came close to using a ruler on both Bobby and Matthew last year, but thankfully it never came to that."

"Sit at your desk." Darryl sat down at one of the desks meant for the youngest students, his knees banging into the desk in front of him.

"Why?"

"I just want to picture you as the teacher." He didn't mention that her hair was falling out of its pins. He could tell that first thing in the morning, she tried to tame her blond curls, but by the end of the day, there were tendrils escaping every which way. He loved it.

Rica sighed, but she sat down at her desk. "School will now come to order," she said in her best teacher voice.

Darryl grinned. "I married the schoolmarm."

"Yes, you really did."

Chapter Four

WHEN THEY ARRIVED AT the teacherage, Darryl was a little dismayed at the tiny little house, but then he realized it would be the perfect place for getting cozy with his new bride. It might even help them to grow closer in more ways than one.

Rica was happy to see that her bed was semi-made. She'd thrown the covers up but hadn't done a good job on it. At least it wasn't completely unmade. The house was not exactly new, but it wasn't old either. It was definitely cozy, made up of a small kitchen area with a table, a sofa, and a bed off in a corner of the room. They would have no privacy, which would be fine when they were a "real" married couple, but for now, it would be difficult for them both.

"It's not much," she said softly, trying to see her small home through his eyes. It was her first home to live in by herself, so she was a bit fonder of it than she probably should have been.

"It's a roof over our heads. I don't come from money, and I don't need anything fancy. This little house will be good for us. I can feel it."

She smiled at that. "Well, thank you for having a positive attitude about it." She frowned at the bed. "We're not going to have any privacy here."

He walked to her, catching her shoulders in his hands and looking into her eyes. "I don't think that's going to bother us. We're newlyweds. Yes, it'll be a little while before we get super close, and when you're ready to change, it'll be easy enough for you to tell me to take a walk."

Rica bit her lip, looking up at him. "That won't bother you?"

Darryl shook his head. "Just say it nicely. I mean, I know there will be times when you want to get rid of me for reasons other than privacy, but if you can pretend it's always for privacy, that would spare my feelings a bit."

She laughed softly. "I will try to always spare your feelings."

"That's kind of you. I'm a lot more . . . well, boisterous than you are. I can see that you're the kind of woman who is content to sit with a book and entertain herself a lot of the time. I'm more gregarious than that. I like to have people around me all the time."

"We'll come up with a compromise that will work for both of us. Are you really willing to have a dance on Friday night at the school?" In other places, she knew they pulled the desks to the side and used the room for dancing. Surely there were some people in town who played instruments and would be happy to play for a dance.

"I really do like the idea. I'll have a sweetheart to dance every dance with. Maybe she'll even let me escort her home and kiss her goodnight."

Rica laughed. "I don't think there will ever be a problem with you kissing me goodnight. I seem to melt every time you touch me."

"Is that so?" he asked, leaning down and pressing his lips to hers. "I like the idea of you melting in my arms."

"Well, I've always been a very serious schoolmarm type, so melting doesn't seem to work well for me. I guess if you promise not to tell anyone, we might be able to do that in private."

He grinned. "Maybe it's not for the best if we talk about melting so much. I need to get ready for bed. I don't think I slept more than four hours per night on that train, and I'm exhausted. I have to work early, and from the sound of it, I'm going to be working awfully hard."

She nodded. "If you'll go for a short walk, I'll change into my nightgown."

"I can do that." He kissed her once more. "I just want to make sure you're still melting while I'm gone."

"There's no doubt about that."

"How long do you need?"

"If you can give me ten minutes, that would be wonderful."

"I'll be back." He shut the door behind him, and she quickly scrambled into her long white nightgown. She hadn't realized when she'd gotten up that morning she would be coming home with a husband.

She asked herself for the hundredth time since she'd agreed to marry him what on earth she was thinking, but truthfully, she knew the answer. He was handsome, kind, funny, and he made her weak in the knees. Was there another reason for marrying a man?

When he came into the cabin ten minutes later, he turned the kerosene lamp down and quickly undressed in the dark. He didn't usually wear more than his underclothes to sleep in, and hopefully she would be all right with that. Otherwise, he was going to have to beg Doris to make him something to wear to not offend his wife's sensibilities.

Climbing into bed beside her, he reached out and pulled her against him. Running a hand up and down her arm, he smiled. "You're so soft, Rica."

She turned onto her side, facing him. "And you're anything but soft." Her hand went to the flat of his chest. "I can tell you're used to doing hard work every day of your life."

"I am, and I have a feeling that's not going to change around here. Not that I'd want it to. I've never been a man who would be content to sit behind a desk every day. My sister Elizabeth's husband was once a Pinkerton agent. He's now a butler, but he still investigates men to see if they are upstanding enough to have a bride sent to him. So, his life is now different, but he still has some adventure involved."

"Do you think you'd enjoy that sort of life?"

Thinking about it for a moment, Darryl shook his head. "No. I like to work with my hands. I once thought what he did was glamorous, but after watching him for a day, I knew I would go insane if I had to do it. I'm meant for manual labor."

"I think I like that about you."

He kissed her quickly. "If we keep touching each other, I'm not going to be content to wait a week."

She immediately moved away from him. "I'm not ready for something more."

"I understand that, which is why I warned you. We'll make it work. I promise." Darryl closed his eyes, exhausted and ready for sleep, but very aware of the beautiful woman lying beside him. His wife.

RICA WOKE BEFORE DAWN the next morning, feeling a heavy weight across her middle. She reached down to lift it off and encountered a rather hairy arm. She froze for just a moment as she realized it was her new husband. Darryl had put his arm around her in his sleep.

She eased out from under the arm and slipped out of bed, dressing in the darkness. Lighting one of her lanterns, she started a fire in the stove, feeling the need to make him a good, hearty breakfast before he went to his first day of work at the mill.

She opened her ice box, removed bacon and eggs, and silently thanked his sister for sending home a loaf of bread with her on Thursday night. She could make toast with eggs and bacon. She had no idea what he liked, but he hadn't seemed like an overly finicky man to her.

When she heard him stirring, she didn't look in his direction, knowing that he'd not slept clothed the night before. Even though he was her husband, she didn't want to accidentally see more than she was ready to see.

Darryl saw Rica already dressed for the day, standing at the stove, making breakfast. He had no idea if she could cook, but he certainly hoped so. If not, he'd just talk Doris into giving her instructions. It was nice to have his twin so close.

He pulled on his pants and walked up behind her, wrapping his arms around her waist and pulling her back against him. "Good morning, Rica."

She smiled and leaned into him. "Good morning, Darryl. Did you sleep all right?"

"I slept like a log. I'm glad I'll have tomorrow off because I will probably need to catch up on some sleep. I've never been quite this tired before."

She frowned a little. "I was thinking we could go on a picnic after church . . ."

"That sounds very nice. We'll have the picnic, and then I'll get a nap afterward. Would that bother you?"

She shook her head. "No, of course not. I know you've traveled a long way and you need to recover."

"Well, it's not like I've been ill, but it does sort of feel like it. I had never been on a train before, and my first trip being two-thousand miles was a bit much for me." His muscles were sore from the unaccustomed inactivity, and he knew he was in for a rough few days as they got used to moving again.

She scooped the eggs onto a plate and added the bacon she'd already done. Opening the oven, she pulled out the toast and set it on his plate as well. "There you are. I hope you like eggs and bacon."

He kissed her quickly after taking the plate. "It looks wonderful. Thank you."

She fixed her own plate and poured them each a cup of coffee. "Are you a coffee drinker?" she asked, holding the cup and looking at him. "I feel like that's something I should already know about the man I married."

He grinned. "I am a coffee drinker, and if we'd courted like normal people, you'd have known it before we married. Remember, we're taking the next week to court each other, so you will know everything you need to know at the end of that week."

"Is that even possible?" she asked, handing him his coffee and sitting down across from him.

"I'm a simple man. How long could it possibly take to know every little detail about me?"

She shook her head. "You think you're a simple man. I have a feeling I'm going to find you a great deal more complicated than you're leading me to believe you are."

"Not possible." He grinned at her, taking her hand in his and bowing his head for a prayer.

After the prayer, she took a bite of her toast. "Do you want children?"

He nodded. "I grew up with thirteen siblings. We ran wild in the countryside of Massachusetts, and I would say I had a truly wonderful childhood. I want to give that to my children."

She choked on her coffee. She knew how many siblings he had, of course, because she was close to his sister, but to hear him talk about it in a discussion about whether he wanted children—well, that was something else entirely. "I hope you don't want fourteen children."

"Good gracious, no! No man in his right mind would ever want fourteen children. He would have to be insane to want that. I'll be content with three or four. It'll be nice that there will be cousins close by for our children to play with."

"Yes, it will. You know it just occurred to me that Doris is *really* my sister now. Gretchen, Doris, and I have been referring to ourselves as Salmon sisters for a while now, so it's fun to think that we're now related."

"I'm happy it pleases you. I've been trying to figure out how not to be her brother for most of my life . . ."

She chose to ignore his comment about not wanting to have Doris for a sister. "It does." She frowned at him. "I have no idea what your tastes in food are. What can I fix for supper that will please you? Anything?"

He shrugged. "Yup. Anything. I'm very easy to please. As long as it's not raw and not burnt, I will gladly eat it. All of my sisters have practiced cooking on me, so I'd probably even eat it raw and burnt."

She grinned at that. "Well, then I will have to test that. I'll go to the store today and get some extra food. I usually eat very simply, and honestly, I take a lot of meals at your sister's house. I'm sure you'll want to do that less than I have been."

"I like my sister. I would love to get to know her kids better. I don't even know the older two boys' names, and it's making me crazy!"

"The oldest is Bobby and the second is Matthew."

"I never thought to even ask you that! Of course you know. You're their teacher!" He shook his head. "Sometimes the brain just doesn't work properly."

She laughed. "I think you're just very tired. And you had an interesting day yesterday. You got off a train and saw your sister for the first time in months, and then you found out the woman you came here to marry wasn't interested in marrying you, and then some other random woman agreed to marry you. That would be a trying day by anyone's standards."

He nodded emphatically. "You're right! I'm excused!"

"Yes, you are." She frowned. "I'm not sure what to pack you for lunch."

"Whatever you usually pack for yourself will work. But more."

"All right." She stood up and went to her ice box, pulling out an apple and some egg salad she'd made up. She quickly spread the egg salad onto two pieces of bread. She put two more pieces of bread on top and wrapped each sandwich in brown paper. She usually had an apple and one sandwich, but she wasn't sure if an apple and two would be enough for him. "Is that enough?"

"Should be. If I'm starving to death, I'll bug Doris." He watched as she put the meal into a tin lunch pail, much like he'd used to carry his lunch to school in back home. "Thank you for making my lunch."

"I'll be more prepared the next time. I promise. I just didn't know I'd be bringing home a husband from my friend's house last night."

"That does rather throw a wrench in things, doesn't it?" He leaned down and brushed his lips across hers. "I'll see you this evening. Are you spending the day with Doris and Gretchen?"

"I'll probably spend the afternoon there. I need to do some shopping this morning. We're going to need a whole lot more food than I usually have on hand." She looked at her stack of papers to be graded on a small table beside the sofa. She would have to take those with her and grade papers while her friends sewed. She'd done it before, and she was always slower because of their chatter, but it was much more enjoyable as well.

"Sounds good. I'll stop by there after work so we can walk home together."

"Can you find your way back?" They'd walked to the teacherage in the dark, and she had no idea how his sense of direction was.

"Yup." With one more kiss, he grabbed his lunch pail and disappeared out the door.

As soon as he was gone, Rica leaned against the counter. The man was already filling every bit of her life. She wondered if she was going to be able to survive him.

Chapter Five

AFTER DOING HER SHOPPING, Rica went to Doris's house, remembering to take the papers she needed to grade. She'd given a history test the day before, and she tried to always get tests back the next school day. Of course, she might not be able to keep up that kind of schedule now that she was married, but she would have a couple of hours every day after school before Darryl came home from work.

When she got to Rica's, Gretchen was already there, sewing away on a shirt for Harv. They'd already completely redone the children's wardrobes, and now they needed to work on Doris's husband's.

"I had to bring work with me," Rica said after Doris opened the door for her. "I gave a test yesterday, and I'm afraid I haven't had time to grade it yet."

"The tests can wait. How did it go last night? Did Darryl really propose on one knee? I just can't picture that!" Doris practically pushed Rica into a chair, ready to get all the details from her friend.

"It went fine. He's a good man. I need to figure out his tastes to cook for him, and it's all so sudden, but I'm going to be a good wife. I've decided." Rica didn't mention the wedding night because she didn't want to admit to her friends she hadn't gone through with it. It was none of their business anyway.

"Did he really propose on one knee? You have to at least tell me that!" Doris insisted.

Rica laughed. "Yes, he did. On the side of the road leading out of town."

"And you said yes. I love it! And we're sisters now!"

Gretchen frowned. "We've all been sisters all along, remember? You're not leaving me out of this!"

Rica grinned at Gretchen. "We're still sisters. I promise. It's just a little more legal with Doris and me."

"I don't care if it's legal as long as we're still sisters of the heart like we've been since the day we all first sat in this kitchen together."

Doris shook her head at Gretchen. "As if that could ever change. It was us against all the women in town for a little while. We have to stick together. There's no choice in the matter!"

"Then that's exactly what we'll do, isn't it?" Gretchen asked.

"Definitely. There's no one else I'd rather stage a coup against the town's bossiest woman with."

WHEN DARRYL STOPPED at Doris's at the end of the day, he found out that Rica had already left. "She didn't want you to have to wait while she cooked supper, so she left a couple of hours ago to get it going for you."

"She's going to be a good wife." Darryl waved at Gretchen, wondering why the girl was a permanent fixture in his sister's kitchen. He liked her well enough, but he knew it was a good thing he had ended up married to Rica instead of her. "I'll see you at church in the morning."

Doris nodded. "Yes, you will. Now go away while I finish fixing our supper." She shut the door in his face, and he laughed.

"Your husband is right behind me!" he called through the door.

"He knows how to open a door!" she yelled back.

Darryl looked at Harv. "She's always been this way. We tried to teach her manners, but they just didn't stick."

Harv smiled. "I love her just the way she is."

"Glad to hear it." Darryl headed toward the teacherage, his mind on his brother-in-law's words. Harv was in love with Doris, which thrilled him for a couple of reasons. He was glad his sister was happy was the first. But the second was more selfish. It told him that a marriage where two people really didn't know each other beforehand really could work. Maybe it wasn't ideal, but it all depended on what he chose to make it. He was very much a man who believed he could choose to love someone. Maybe he wasn't in love with his wife yet, but he would be. Because he chose to love, and he chose to be happy.

When he got to the teacherage, it seemed strange to just walk in, but it was his home now. He opened the door and called out to her, so she'd not be nervous. "Rica! I'm home!"

She turned from the stove and smiled at him. "Are you always this noisy when you get home at the end of a long day of work?"

He shrugged. "No idea. Until yesterday, I lived with my family on the farm I grew up on. This is all new to me."

"Well, I'm glad you're having the new life with me. It's strange to me to have someone live with me after being here alone."

"How long have you been here?" Darryl asked, setting his lunch pail on the counter and sinking into one of the kitchen chairs.

"This is my second year. I was here for the fall and spring semesters last year, and then I went home for the summer. Now I'm back. So I've been here a year but only part of a year." She pulled a loaf of bread from the oven and set it on the counter. "I hope you're hungry. I made a pork roast, mashed potatoes and gravy, carrots, and fresh bread."

"It all smells wonderful. Are you always going to spoil me this way?"

She laughed. "Don't count on it. I get so involved in grading papers, I might forget to cook at times. I'll do my best."

"That's all I can ask. Didn't you say that to the boys yesterday?"

"Yes, I did. And I meant it." Rica served the food onto two plates. "How was your first day working with Harv?"

"It's a good thing I'm used to hard work because he wasn't kidding about how behind he is. I learned a lot of new things today. I think I'll enjoy the job, but it's a lot to get used to."

"I can't imagine that working in a sawmill would be easy work." She set the plates on the table and filled two glasses with milk.

"It's not, but that's all right. I'll be a little sore as I get used to the new motions. My body is strong, but it's farmer strong. It's going to have to get sawmill strong."

"Is the wage fair?" she asked.

He laughed. "You know, we still haven't talked about a wage. I should maybe discuss that with him. We just jumped into work, and with as loud as the saw is all day, it's hard to actually talk to each other."

"It's still information you might want to have. A teacher's pay isn't great, but with a house being furnished, it's a lot better than it could be. If I didn't love it so much, I don't know that I could continue."

As they ate, he talked about what the job had entailed. "I was surprised you weren't at my sister's when I got there at the end of the day. I thought we'd decided you were going to walk home with me."

"Yes, but then I realized I wouldn't be able to have supper ready if we did that, and I really wanted to fix a nice meal on our first night as husband and wife. Well, the first night I cooked for you."

"Did you get all your papers graded?"

She nodded. "I did. I have to plan lessons for this week yet, but if you're really going to take a nap tomorrow, I'll have plenty of time then."

"I probably will take a nap. It's not something I usually do, but I feel like I should be my best for my job, and I won't be while I'm sleep-deprived."

Rica smiled at that. "I admire your work ethic."

Darryl laughed. "Is that because it's so similar to yours?"

"Probably. I'm glad I married a man who understands hard work and cares so much about doing what's right for his employer. I can't imagine being married to someone who doesn't give his all one hundred percent of the time."

"I think you'll find we agree on things like that."

"Good. That matters a lot to me." After supper, Rica did the dishes while he rested on the sofa, talking to her the whole while.

"Do you want me to help fix supper some nights?"

Rica shook her head. "I don't think so. Do you know how to cook?"

"No earthly idea. I just thought it would be nice to offer." He watched her move efficiently. "I can help with dishes some nights."

"Did you help with kitchen chores at home?"

"Oh, no. My parents were very old-fashioned about things like that. The girls helped out in the house while the boys did stuff outside. I milked cows, helped in the fields, and all that sort of thing. My sisters kept the house clean and cooked and minded the younger children."

"So do you even know how to wash dishes?" she asked.

"Well, no, but I could learn. I'm learning how to work at a sawmill."

"I'll do the dishes. If I get sick, I'll probably ask for help, though."

"That sounds fair. If I get sick, I will not ask you to help at the sawmill." He grinned at the idea. "Do you ever wear your hair down?"

She blinked a bit at the change of subject. "No, it's unruly. I look much more schoolteachery with it up."

"I've been daydreaming about pulling all those pins from your hair to watch your curls fall since the moment I met you."

"Even when you thought you were going to marry Gretchen?" Rica asked. She was very surprised to hear him say that because she'd never known a man to think about her in any way other than impersonally.

"Yes. I was already feeling bad that I'd be marrying your friend and thinking about you, but what's a man to do? I made a promise. I'm so glad it worked out the way it did."

She put the last dish up and walked over to join him on the sofa. "I can't believe you've been thinking about my hair that way."

"Trust me, I have." He reached out and wrapped his arm around her shoulders. "Your hair is very beautiful. Sexy even."

"You do know who you're talking to, don't you?" Rica felt like in his mind she was transformed into someone else.

"Definitely." He turned toward her on the sofa, his free hand reaching for her hair. "May I?"

She blushed but nodded. If he wanted to see her hair down so badly, she didn't have a problem with it. "Yes, of course. You're my husband." She belonged to him. Whether she believed it should be that way or not, she knew the laws of the land, and she knew that legally she was his in every way.

He removed each pin he saw and watched as her hair cascaded down around her shoulders. When he thought he was finished, he ran his fingers through her hair and found a couple of more pins. "Will you wear your hair down for me at home?" He pulled one strand of hair straight and found that it was much longer than it seemed.

She nodded. "If you want me to. Do you really like my hair that much?"

Darryl couldn't even believe she was asking him that. Had no man ever told her how beautiful her hair was before? "Yes! There's just something about it. When your hair is all pinned to the top of your head that way, you seem like the perfect schoolteacher. Then I take it down and . . . well, you don't look like a schoolmarm anymore."

"Is that a good thing or a bad thing?"

He shrugged. "I enjoy the pretty schoolmarm, but I think it's going to be very easy to love the beautiful girl who cooks wonderful meals for me." He ran his fingers through her hair, thoroughly enjoying how it felt against his skin. "Do you have to braid it for bed? Or can you sleep with it free?"

She laughed. "You're obsessed."

"Probably. Can you sleep with it free?"

She shook her head. "If I did that it would take me an hour to brush it out every morning."

"I could brush it for you . . ."

"Have you ever done that?"

"Only once. Doris got gum stuck in her hair. Ma was too busy to mess with it, so I brushed it out for her. But she's my sister. I know I would feel very differently brushing your hair."

"If you really want to, I'll let you do it sometime." To her, her hair was just another chore. Something else she had to do every day to look like the proper schoolteacher. It was obviously something very different to him.

"Really? Where's your hairbrush?"

"Now?" She bit her lip, a little surprised that he seemed so interested in brushing her hair.

"Now. I know it seems strange, but your hair fascinates me. It was the first thing I noticed about you, and I was immediately attracted."

"All right." She got up and walked across the cabin to the dresser. Her brush was laying on top of it. She picked it up and carried it back to him.

He had her sit on the floor at his feet, and he carefully stroked the brush over her hair. She leaned her head forward and felt tingles through her body as he pulled it through her curls over and over. "How many strokes do you do?"

"One hundred every night," she said. She hated brushing her hair, but there was something very sensual about what he was doing.

"Maybe we can make this our nighttime ritual. Every night I'll do the one hundred strokes for you." He loved the idea of getting his hands on her hair every single night. Maybe it was strange, but he didn't care.

"I guess. To me it's just another chore."

"Oh, trust me. It's so much more to me than that." He finally stopped and handed her the hairbrush, surprised at how very aroused he was. "I'm going to go for my walk. I'll be back in ten minutes." He needed some cold night air to be able to get into bed with her.

Rica got up off the floor and stared at the door he'd closed behind him. She felt like something special had just happened, and she just wished she understood exactly what it meant.

Chapter Six

SUNDAY WAS A BIT ODD for Rica. At church, people she barely knew were coming over for an introduction to Darryl. She saw looks in some of the mamas' eyes, telling her they were thinking of him for a daughter. Many of the young ladies of town came over to get an introduction, only to see their faces fall when she introduced him as her husband.

Darryl took it all in calmly. He stayed close to Rica, wishing the other young ladies in town would realize he was taken. He'd never had so many women interested in him, which made sense because everyone in Beckham knew him. Here he was a stranger.

As Rica watched it all, she couldn't help but wonder if he was regretting their hasty marriage. She'd experimented with a new hairstyle that morning, which allowed many of the tendrils of her hair to fall freely, which she knew he liked, but there were certainly other women in town who he would prefer to spend his life with.

After church, he slipped his arm around her waist as they left the building. "I'm glad that's over. I felt like a piece of meat at auction in there!" he said as they walked away.

Rica laughed aloud. "You certainly have a way with words, Darryl. Have you ever thought of being a writer?"

"Me? A writer? I think the world would open up and suck me inside if I ever contemplated something like that. It's against the natural order of things for certain." What a thought. A man like he was couldn't do anything intellectual like writing. He was meant to work with his hands.

She walked toward a meadow where she'd once seen a man and woman picnicking, knowing that's where she wanted their picnic to be.

It had been in the spring, just before school let out for the year, and ever since, she hadn't been able to walk by the meadow without thinking of doing the same. "I think you could do it. Your natural language makes me think of poetry."

He shook his head. "I think you have me confused with your other husband. Where is he?"

"Excuse me?" she asked, very confused.

"The husband you have me confused with. I will need to find him and strangle him. I'm a one-woman man, and I need a woman who feels the same about me." He winked at her, making her blush.

"You are a crazed lunatic at times, Darryl Miller. How did I get so lucky as to have you in my life?" She stopped in the middle of the meadow and opened the picnic basket, removing the quilt she'd added. As she smoothed it out, she thought about making a special quilt for their bed. She wanted something pretty now that she didn't live alone. She was amazed at how much more she cared about little details, now that she was sharing her life with Darryl.

"I'm the lucky one."

As soon as they were sitting in the middle of the quilt, she carefully unpacked their lunch. She'd made fried chicken, potato salad, and chocolate cookies. She also had a big jar of lemonade. Fixing their plates, she handed one to him.

"Thank you for making lunch for us," he said softly. "You make me feel like I'm the most important man in the world, and I've never felt that way." He leaned toward her, cupping her cheek with one hand, kissing her softly. Without warning he plucked a few of the pins from her hair, watching some of it fall to her shoulders in a cascade of curls. "Have I ever told you how very much I love your hair?"

She laughed softly. "Please don't ever touch my hair until after four on schooldays. I have this feeling that you will never be content unless my hair is sticking every which way."

"You're right. I've never been mesmerized by a woman's hair before, but there's something about yours that really makes me a little bit crazy. I want to spend all my time touching it, and brushing it, and just looking at it."

"If you're trying to make me feel courted and admired, you're doing a very good job of it."

He grinned. "Of course I want you to feel that way, but I'm not doing anything special to make it happen. I'm just acting like I naturally act with a beautiful woman beside me."

She felt her heart give a little flutter as she smiled at him. "You, Darryl Miller, are good for my self-esteem. I don't think I've ever had a man interested in me in all my twenty-five years, and now I sit here with you, basking in the attention of a very handsome man. I worried at church today that you would regret our marriage with so many beautiful young ladies to choose from, but you seem to be content with me. I'm not sure why, but I am grateful that God sent you into my life."

He reached forward and rubbed his thumb across her bottom lip. "I know we're doing everything sort of backwards, but I don't ever want you to think I wouldn't have chosen you if given a chance. I was attracted to you immediately, and I would have liked a chance to know you before marriage, but we can make it work now."

"I hope so." She was still worried about it, and she wasn't sure why. Probably because of the interest the other women had shown in him at church. If he was a sought-after man, why would he choose her?

"Look at Harv and Doris. They married even sooner after they met than you and I did. And they're happy. Harv told me yesterday that he loves Doris and wouldn't change her. I can see on Doris's face that she loves him. If those two can make it work with four children involved, we can make it work with just the two of us."

Rica shrugged. "Maybe they were able to make it work *because* of the children. Maybe the children added another dimension to the whole thing that made them want to make it work more, so they tried harder. Is that possible?"

Darryl looked at her. "No one wants a marriage to work more than I do at this moment. I think you're an incredible woman, Rica Miller, and I want us to look back in a few months and wonder what we ever worried about in the beginning."

She smiled. "I need to remember that we're both fully invested in our marriage. It's not just one of us needing to make it work. It's two."

"Three."

She frowned at him. "Three?"

"I believe God is in our marriage as well—a cord made with three strands is stronger than one made with only two. Don't you think? We'll use that cord to tie us together for the rest of our lives."

She smiled and unwrapped a small pile of cookies from a cloth napkin. "For that, you get a cookie!"

He laughed. "Anything for cookies!"

After they had cleaned up their picnic, they walked back toward the teacherage. "I hope there aren't any problems with my job now that I'm married. In a lot of areas, teachers aren't allowed to marry during their term, but that's not part of my contract here."

"Are you worried about it?" he asked.

"Not really, but there are some women in this town who would do anything to make my life difficult. I just hope none of them are on the school board." She was thinking of Mrs. Lindon. The older woman caused her enough trouble just by sending her children to school.

"Hopefully not. I don't know where we'd live if that happened, but we'd figure it out. Do you plan to continue teaching for a long time?" He knew eventually he'd have to sort out permanent housing for them, but he wanted to know how soon.

Rica shrugged. "Until children come along probably. I don't see being able to keep working after I have them, but I would love to work up until they're born."

He nodded. "That works for me. If the school board tries to fight you, we'll fight back." He opened the door to the teacherage and let her precede him inside. "Are you really all right with me taking a nap? I know we're trying to spend time together today, but I'm so tired!"

"Of course. I'll do my lesson plans for the week while you sleep. You need to be able to work tomorrow."

He leaned down and kissed her, his fingers automatically winding through her hair and plucking out the rest of the pins. He held out his hands, palm up, with all of the pins in them. "Oops."

Rica took the pins and walked over to put them on her dresser. "Oops? I think that was a little more deliberate than an oops." She picked up her bag where she kept her school books and opened it. "I'll be as quiet as I can. If I make too much noise rustling papers around, I can go to the school and work there."

"Did you talk to people about the school dance on Friday night?" he asked as he removed his shirt. He'd sleep in his pants to keep from offending her delicate sensibilities, but she could deal with seeing him shirtless.

"I did. I even got Mrs. Gottweiler to put up a sign on the bulletin board at the mercantile. We're going to have cookies and cakes, punch, and lots of dancing. She told me there's a group of men in town who love to play their instruments together, and she's going to get that arranged. I'll have my students make decorations for the dance, and we'll start it at seven sharp."

"You've done a lot of work for it. I can't wait to dance with my beautiful bride." He walked over and kissed her once more before lying down. "I like being able to grab you and kiss you whenever I feel like it. It makes me happy."

Before Rica could figure out how to respond to that, he was already asleep. She frowned at him for a moment before turning to her work. Having him around was certainly making life more interesting. Only two days with him, and already she couldn't figure out if her heartbeat would ever return to normal.

She worked for an hour steadily before getting up and starting supper. She wanted him to be able to eat as soon as he was hungry. She was making extra as well, so she could send him to work with a good lunch the next day.

It had never occurred to her that she would someday be managing a career and a husband, but she was doing it now. Her marriage came first, of course, but her pupils were almost as important to her. She knew other women were able to do it, and she would do it, too.

As soon as her supper was cooking, she sat back down at the table and wrote a letter to her parents. They were expecting her to come home the next weekend, and she didn't feel like it was a good time with being newly married. And of course her parents weren't yet aware of her marriage. The letter she wrote explained that she'd married suddenly, but that she was happy. She would come home in a few weeks once she and Darryl had settled into married life a bit better.

She folded the letter, hoping her parents would understand. She knew her mother would, but her father had always been a little less understanding than she would have preferred. She guessed his reaction truly didn't matter because there was nothing he could do about it now.

She was above the age of consent by a long way, and she was content being married to her Darryl. Hopefully someday they would realize they loved one another, and she could be truly happy. It sounded like a fairy tale ending to her, and she wasn't one to believe in fairy tales, but she would hope and dream.

She settled down to read a novel, curled up on the couch. Sundays had always been novel-reading days for her, though she had to keep her novels hidden in case someone came by. Schoolteachers were not to read frivolous literature like novels, but sometimes she just didn't care. Shakespeare was all well and good, but give her one of the Bronte sisters any day.

Even her mother didn't know of her penchant for novel reading, and she'd have been scandalized if she had. Never mind, though, because the novels kept Rica's mind filled with laughter and thoughts of love, while the common every day works of literature she used for lessons with her students didn't.

Without the novels, she would never have had the courage to marry a stranger—even if he was the twin brother of one of her closest friends. It was hard to believe that she was now in a marriage and a courtship at the same time. They really were doing things backwards, but she had hope because she had read novels. Maybe that wasn't something she should be proud of, but having courage was something foreign to her. She'd married a stranger, and she was going to do everything she could to make the very most of it.

Chapter Seven

MONDAY MORNING, RICA was up a bit earlier than usual to make a good breakfast for her and Darryl. She usually just had toast or something equally easy, but she was certain that wouldn't sustain him through hours of hard, physical labor.

As soon as breakfast was ready, she woke him. She hated that he didn't have a little more time to rest before starting his full work schedule, but she understood where Harv was coming from as well, needing the help desperately.

Darryl woke up to see his beautiful wife standing over him. Her hair was still down, and he smiled at her. "An angel waking me in the morning. I think I've died and gone to heaven."

She laughed. "You're silly. It's time to wake up. You need to be at work in an hour. I have your lunch made, and your breakfast is ready."

"And coffee? Did you make plenty of coffee? I might need a few gallons to make it through the day." Why couldn't he spend another week in bed with his beautiful bride?

"I made a pot of coffee, not gallons."

His hand whipped out from under the covers and pulled her down into bed with him. "I won't muss you, because your hair isn't fixed yet."

She grinned. "But your breakfast might get cold." Not that she minded at that moment.

"There is that . . ." He pulled her head down for a kiss, running his hands up and down her sides. She was still in her nightgown and a robe, and he liked how she looked that way—she wasn't the proper teacher and instead was just Rica, his very kissable wife.

She sighed and sank into him, enjoying the kiss more than she really should have. She was starting to wonder if she was a wanton woman with as much as she enjoyed him, but then she realized that she was worrying too much. She needed to just let things happen as they would.

"Wait . . . did you say coffee and breakfast were ready? What are you doing lying on top of me? Get off me!"

She shook her head at him as she got up, walking to the stove to pour his coffee. Sometimes she had no idea to react to his teasing. It was odd, but no one in her life had ever teased her. Not even her brother. He was two years younger than her, and they'd treated each other with politeness, not teasing. After watching the way Darryl was with Doris, she could see that he had never even thought to not tease his sisters.

After he'd finished his breakfast, Darryl got to his feet, pulling her to hers. "I don't want to leave you. Do you think I could talk Harv and the school district into giving us each about three months off? We could just gaze into each other's eyes."

"You don't think that even that exciting event would get boring after a while?"

He shrugged. "Not for me. You have the most beautiful eyelashes I've ever seen. They're so long and thick. I look into your eyes, and I feel like I'm completely losing myself."

She stepped back into his arms and held him tightly. "You are a truly good man. Thank you for coming into my life."

He grinned, grabbed his lunch from the counter, and headed out the door. "I'll be home as soon as my evil brother-in-law releases me from my bondage!"

She grinned as he left, closing the door behind him. He really did bring excitement to her otherwise-dull world. She hoped she wouldn't realize it was *too* much excitement as time went by.

Once the dishes were done and the cabin was neat and tidy, she took her books to the schoolhouse. The children started to get there around eight most mornings, though school didn't start until nine. She did her best to always be the first person there, available for any of the children who felt like they needed extra help.

That particular morning, she sat at her desk, going over her lesson plans and making certain she was ready for the day. They would start their art project that included making decorations for the dance the next day, and she planned to announce to the children there would be a dance after lunch. She knew they'd be excited—especially the older children.

As she read over her history lesson, one of the older girls came into the schoolhouse, and she didn't notice her until the girl said her name. "Miss Hughes?"

Rica looked up and smiled. "Yes? How can I help you, Gloria?" The girl was sixteen and one of her best students. She enjoyed talking to her when there was time.

"Could I ask you something?"

"Of course." Rica frowned at the girl, wondering what her topic of conversation was that she was starting out that way. Usually Gloria didn't have a problem asking whatever was on her mind.

"Mr. Jackson has asked my mother if he can court me, and my mother said yes. He has six children, and his wife died last year. Do you know him?"

Rica shook her head. "None of his children come here, do they?"

"No, ma'am. His oldest is a ten-year-old girl, and she has to stay home and take care of the other children. From what I understand, she's expected to do all the cooking and cleaning."

"That's terrible!"

"I think so, too," Gloria said. "Anyway, Mr. Jackson is going to take me out driving after school, and I really don't want to go, but my ma keeps telling me that this is a good opportunity for me. I should be pleased that a man his age wants to court me and possibly marry me. She thinks I'm too 'bookish' and that no man would ever want to marry me as a result."

Rica frowned at that. "I've always been a book lover. If I have a spare minute or two, my nose is buried in a book, and I'm reading as many pages as I can until I'm forced to return to reality. Did you know I got married on Friday afternoon?"

Gloria shook her head. "No, ma'am."

"Well, I did. I married a wonderful man who has no problem at all with how much I enjoy reading. If you wait for a man who suits you and don't marry the first man that comes along, I think you'll be happier in the long run."

"But how do I convince my mother of that? She's certain that I'll die an old maid if I don't allow Mr. Jackson to court me. But he's an old man. At least thirty-five!"

Rica smiled at her student's idea of what constituted old. "Would your mother be amenable to a visit from me to discuss things with her? I don't want to interfere, but I can't imagine you being happy getting married right away. You need to go to college. You're the kind of girl who would thrive surrounded by books for the rest of her life."

"I think so, too, but make sure you don't say that to my mother. I think she would have a heart attack at the idea of me going off to school. She wants me to be under her thumb for the rest of my life, having babies and just being an obedient daughter, I guess." Gloria frowned as she looked down at her hands. "I've always been obedient to my mother. I do what she tells me with no hesitation or question. But I don't want to be courted—and especially not by an old man."

"I can understand that, Gloria. Don't worry. If your mother will receive me, I'll be certain to talk to her." Rica wasn't certain she'd be able to get through to her, but she thought she could. She said a silent prayer, thanking God for sending her a mother who understood her so well.

"I'll ask her tonight." Gloria got to her feet. "I always appreciate you taking the time to talk to me, Miss Hughes. It's like you think I'm an adult and worthy of your respect. No one else seems to feel that way."

"Well, I really do. We'll make sure you don't have to marry old Mr. Jackson." Rica watched as the teenager left the schoolhouse to go and wait outside with all the others. She wanted to slap the girl's mother for making it seem like she was less for not courting. Marriage wasn't what everyone wanted, and someday women would be able to make all their own decisions. She just wished that someday was now.

She stood to write her new name on the blackboard. She hadn't thought to do it until right that minute, but Gloria had called her Miss Hughes. It would take her a bit to be able to respond to Mrs. Miller, but it was her new name, and it made her heart flutter a bit, thinking about what had given her the name.

After lunchtime that day, she made her announcement. "On Friday evening this week, we're going to have a dance, right here at the school. All of you need to bring anything you think you can use to make decorations for the dance."

"Why are we having a dance, Miss Hughes?" Peter, the boy who asked, blushed. "I mean, Mrs. Miller."

"Because I've never been involved in a dance in this community. Most communities do more things together than this one, and now that I'm married, I'm going to do my best to help people here become tighter knit."

Molly, the youngest of Mrs. Lindon's children, raised her hand. "My ma says you and your friends are troublemakers, and you want nothing more than to change Salmon into something that no one here wants. Is that true?"

It was all Rica could do to continue smiling at the child, forcing herself to remember that she couldn't take out her anger with Molly's mother on the girl. "It is not true. My friends and I want Salmon to be a good, welcoming place for anyone to live. We're working hard to help it become just that."

Molly shrugged. "Are students allowed to go to the dance?"

Rica smiled and nodded. "It's my hope that everyone in town will attend the dance. There's no cost to get in, but we are asking everyone bring either a plate of cookies or a cake to share."

"My mother bakes the best cakes in all of Oregon. Maybe the whole world!" Bobby said. It was out of turn, but Rica couldn't argue with him. Doris made wonderful baked goods.

"Then you're going to have to make sure that she sends a cake for us!"

"Are you and Uncle Darryl going to be at the dance?" Matthew asked.

Rica nodded. "Yes, we are. I hope your parents will be there as well."

"Are you going to kiss Uncle Darryl in front of everyone like you did at your wedding?" Bobby asked.

She gave him her sternest look as all of the children giggled. "I'm married to your uncle now, but we won't be talking about the two of us kissing during school—or at any other time for that matter." She turned to the board and wrote down an arithmetic problem. She needed the children to concentrate on school again, and she needed her cheeks to stop flaming red.

As soon as school was out, Gloria came to the front of the class again, lingering and making it clear she was waiting for the other students to leave so she could have a private talk with Rica. "Would you mind sending a letter home with me, so you could ask my ma if you could stop by? She'd like that better than me asking her if you can. She likes things to be done all proper like."

"I'd be happy to. Just give me a minute, and I'll write the note for you." Rica pulled a clean sheet of paper from her notebook and quickly wrote the note in her perfect handwriting. "There you go. Tell her I'm happy to meet with her, whenever is convenient for her."

As the girl took the note and hurried away, Rica cleaned the blackboard and walked through the school to make sure the students had left everything tidy, endeavoring to sweep every corner. It was her job to make sure the schoolroom was clean at all times, after all.

After she had finished, she walked over to Doris's house, wanting to ask her advice about Gloria's situation. She couldn't actually mention Gloria's name, but if she could find out a little more about Mr. Jackson, she would feel as if she was better equipped for the upcoming conversation with Gloria's mother.

Doris had obviously been watching for her because as she raised her hand to knock, the door was opened, and she was pulled inside. "You were seen picnicking in the meadow with my brother. And I hear there were at least a few kisses exchanged . . ."

Rica shook her head at Doris. "Do you have spies everywhere?" She looked over at Gretchen, who was sewing and trying not to laugh. "Hi, Gretchen!"

"How was school today?" Gretchen asked, giving Rica an out from the interrogation Doris obviously had planned.

"It was good. I talked to the children about the dance on Friday night. I'm really getting excited about it." Rica sat down across from Gretchen, reaching for one of the cookies in the middle of the table. Doris really did make the best baked goods.

"We haven't had a dance here in town in . . . I can't remember how long! I wasn't old enough that my mother would allow me to go with an escort, though. I had to go with her and Papa, and I had to stay beside them. Reginald asked me to dance one time, and neither of my parents were pleased, but at least they didn't stop us."

Rica covered Gretchen's hand with her own. "It must be really hard for you."

Gretchen shrugged, ignoring the tear that coursed down her cheek. "I always knew I'd marry him. It was like the moment we met, we knew our souls were meant to live as one. We were inseparable at school and would have been the rest of the time if our parents had allowed it."

"I'm so sorry you lost him." Rica hadn't ever really thought about the man behind Gretchen's condition. Yes, she knew his name, but thinking of him as Gretchen saw him—she couldn't imagine the pain the other girl was going through. She was already falling in love with Darryl after just a few days. Reginald and Gretchen had years together.

Gretchen smiled. "As my mother tells me every single day, I can't bury myself with him. Especially not with a baby on the way."

Doris sat down at the table with them and grabbed a cookie of her own. "Have you thought about what you're going to do when the baby comes? Can you stay in the house with your mother then?"

Gretchen shrugged. "I'm going to have to. I don't have anywhere else to go. I'm hoping Mother takes one look at her grandchild and falls in love with him. Stranger things have happened."

"I hope so, too." Doris smiled at Gretchen, and then her eyes met Rica's. They both knew it was unlikely, but what could they do? Gretchen was making the choice to stay there.

Rica sighed. "I have a question for you both. Do either of you know a Mr. Jackson with six children who lost his wife last year?"

Gretchen wrinkled her nose. "As soon as Reginald died, he asked to court me. His wife hadn't been dead for four months. He's a horrible man. I think his wife killed herself just to get away from him."

"Really? That's awful!"

"You should smell him. And his breath. Everyone says that his daughter, who just turned ten, is taking care of the house, doing all the cooking, and taking care of her younger siblings. He's asked out every eligible woman here in Salmon, and now rumor has it he's taken to trying to court some of the schoolgirls. Gloria was seen talking to him at her house last week, and everyone thinks her mother is going to make her court him."

Rica didn't want to admit that was true, but it sounded like Gretchen already knew exactly what was going on anyway. How she always knew so much when so few people would talk to her always surprised Rica. "Gloria talked to me before school today. Her mother is making her go for a drive with him because she's afraid that Gloria is going to be an old maid because she reads too much." Rica took off her spectacles and rubbed her eyes. "Gloria is my very brightest student. If anyone could go to college, it would be her, and that's what she wants. Of course, all her mother wants for her is marriage."

Gretchen frowned. "Sounds like another Salmon mother is trying to control the lives of her children. I had a feeling it was happening. I didn't know Gloria was so bright, though. She was a few grades behind me in school."

"I'm going to talk to her mother, and I hope it will help, but I have this horrible feeling it won't. I don't want to go to school on Monday morning to find out my best student has been forced to marry a man she doesn't like so she can help him raise a houseful of children. She's too young! She has too much promise!" Rica felt tears of frustration pop into her eyes. How could she change the world one student at a time when their parents were always fighting against her?

"You have to at least try," Doris responded. "You care too much to do anything else."

"I do. I wish I didn't, but how do I stop myself from caring about every single student?"

Chapter Eight

DARRYL STOPPED ON HIS way home from work that day to pick some of the wildflowers growing in the meadow where they'd picnicked. He knew his Rica would love them, and he needed her to be happy. He wondered just how much longer they would be in the courting portion of their relationship. He didn't know about her, but he was more than ready to move on.

When he walked in the door with a bouquet of flowers in his hand, he put his lunch pail on the counter and walked over to where she was stirring a soup on the stove. "I thought of you today," he said as he planted a kiss on the side of her neck.

Rica smiled at him, but the smile was distant. "I thought of you, too!"

"Are you all right? You look like something's wrong."

She thought about talking to him about Gloria and Mr. Jackson, but she wasn't sure if she should be bringing her troubles home. They were barely married. Shouldn't she be trying to keep things light and positive at home? "I'm fine. Just a little tired. The children are very excited about making the decorations for the dance."

He frowned, knowing there was more to it, but not sure how to get her to talk to him about whatever it was. "I brought you these." He handed her the flowers with a flourish, and Rica took them with a big smile. Whatever had been bothering her seemed to disappear the instant she saw the flowers.

"Thank you!" Tears popped into her eyes, and she felt silly as she found a glass to put the flowers in.

"What's wrong? Why did flowers make you cry?" He had never been able to understand why women seemed to cry at the littlest things, but he wanted to make sure his Rica wasn't sad.

"No one has ever brought me flowers. I thought they'd look beautiful in a vase, but then I realized I didn't have a vase because no one has ever brought me flowers. It makes me sad that no one has ever thought to do something so sweet for me before, and then I think of all the women in the world who have never had anyone bring them flowers, and it makes me cry for them. Because everyone should have that single moment of sheer delight when they're handed flowers by someone who is special to them."

"You thought all that in the three seconds from when I handed you the flowers until you turned?" He was utterly amazed that anyone could think all of that so fast. His wife was awfully special.

She nodded. "It's a curse."

"I'd call it a blessing. It means you have a huge heart, and you have a capacity to care about others that most people have no idea about. I think it makes me care about you even more."

Care. Not love. She loved him. Did he not love her in return? She turned her back on him and continued stirring the soup. It didn't need to be stirred any longer, but she needed a moment with him unable to see her face.

When she put their supper on the table, he filled their glasses with milk, feeling like he was walking on eggshells. He'd upset her tonight, but he wasn't sure how. He didn't want her to be sad. He wanted to only fill her life with love and goodness.

"How was work today?" she asked softly. She needed to get her mind back to the present and quit worrying about whether or not he loved her. She also had to get Gloria out of her mind. Worrying would never solve anything.

"It was good. Busy as busy can be. I was able to free up Harv to sit down and actually get some invoices written out. He's been so busy with the next project, he hadn't been able to do that for a while. I honestly think we still need a third man to help us, but we're holding our own. Not catching up, but I don't think that's going to happen."

"Are you enjoying the work?"

"I really am. I know it's not sitting around and thinking all day like what you do, but I was able to work with my hands, and I felt good at the end of the day. I like to put in a hard day's work." Darryl knew he should probably aspire to be more, but he did what made him happy. He hoped she didn't think less of him for that.

"I'm glad it's working out for you. I was a little afraid you'd hate it. You took quite a risk leaving everything you knew to move here and take on a job doing something you'd never done before."

"I needed to take a risk. I've done the same thing every day of my life. Well, since I got out of school, but I only went to school for a few months out of the year as well. I hope that makes sense."

She nodded emphatically. "I have never in my life done anything impulsively until I met you. Everything was always thought about and considered, and every risk was measured. I feel so good about doing something that was out of my comfort zone."

"You do?"

"Yes! I even wrote to my parents. I was supposed to go home this coming weekend, but with the dance, I thought I needed to stay. So I wrote to them and told them I'd married and my husband works Saturdays, so they'd know that I wouldn't be heading back home any weekend soon."

He frowned at her. "I want to meet your family."

"Don't worry. You will. I know my father is going to love you. He's a carpenter, and he thinks men are only real men if they work with their hands." Rica grinned. "My mother will just be happy that I found someone who makes me happy."

He took her hand in his. "Do I make you happy, Rica?"

"After a full seventy-two hours of marriage, I can honestly say you do. Now in a month or two that answer might change . . ." Her eyes twinkled as she teased him.

"What happened today to make you sad?" he asked, determined to know why she'd looked so unhappy when he'd come in the door. He knew she was a great deal more serious than he was, but he was used to her being a bit more upbeat.

She sighed. "One of my students came to me today and told me that her mother is making her allow an older man in the community to court her. He's a widower with six small children, and her mother thinks she should be open to marrying him. According to Gretchen, he smells bad."

Darryl frowned. "Why would her mother do that? My parents had fourteen children, and my mother cried when every one of us moved out. She tried to hide it, but she'd have red-rimmed eyes for days." He smiled for a moment. "I bet she secretly rejoices when the youngest Ida Mae finally leaves."

"This girl is very intelligent. In fact, I think she has a good chance at getting a college scholarship if she wants one. Her mother thinks she's too studious and she will never find a man if she doesn't marry this one. You'd be surprised at how much mothers tend to worry about girls who don't spend all their time worried about their appearance and which beau will take them out on Saturday night."

"Now I understand. There are different expectations for boys and girls. If a boy studies hard, he can be anything he wants. A doctor, a lawyer, even a banker. If a girl does the same, people worry that she'll never marry. A woman is judged by the man she marries. A man is only judged on his own merit. It's wrong, but it's how our world is."

"So if we have a daughter who walks around reading all the time and never pays any attention to what she wears, you'll let her be? If she wants to be a doctor, you'll help her reach that goal?"

"Yes, I will. I'd love to go talk to this girl's mother because someone needs to talk some sense into her. How could she really think that her daughter would be better off with a man that much older than her who would expect her to raise his children?"

"You know, if she had seen him at church, and they'd started up a flirtation, and she was interested in him, I'd still have reservations, but I wouldn't try to stop it. But this situation is totally different. The girl told me that she spoke to her mother and told her that she didn't want to let this man court her, and her mother told her she had no choice." Rica shook her head. "In this day and age, we're beyond arranged marriages! Women should be able to choose who they want to marry, not agree to marry whoever their mother finds for them." She stood up, starting to clear the table. She hadn't eaten more than a few bites, but she was too upset to do so.

Darryl watched her for a few minutes, realizing how genuinely upset she was with the situation. She wanted to help, but really all she could do was talk to the other woman, and if she was told to mind her own business, then that's what she'd have to do. She deeply cared about her students and more than just academically.

He wanted badly to fix the situation for her, but there was truly nothing he could do. He was simply the husband of the schoolteacher, and he had no say and no clout in the community. It wasn't as bad as Beckham, but it was still not what he wanted from life.

He walked to the sofa and watched her work. When she'd finished, she walked over to sit with him, her head on his shoulder. He'd just put in an eleven-hour day at work, and she'd complained to him when he came home at the end of the day. "I'm really sorry I talked to you about the situation. You shouldn't have to hear about my petty troubles at the end of your day."

Darryl cupped her face in his hands. "I wish I could fix all of your troubles for you. You have the right to tell me anything bad that happens. I'm here to listen. We're partners in life. Everything we do should be to help build that partnership. If you don't talk to me about your troubles, I won't have a real place in your life."

She blinked at him, still having a hard time believing this caring man was her husband. "You really feel that way?"

"I really do." He leaned down to brush his lips across hers, and she felt the familiar spark start in her stomach.

His fingers went to her hair, and the next thing she knew her hair was down around her shoulders again. "I'm so sorry!"

He frowned. "What are you sorry about?" She hadn't done anything to apologize for.

"I was planning on making sure my hair was down before you came home from work every night. I didn't, and I should have." Rica shook her head.

"Why should you have?"

"Because you like it down. It's something simple enough I can do for you to make you happy, so I should do it."

He frowned. "Only if it makes you happy, too. I love your hair down, but you have a choice in how you wear it. I just like pulling the pins out and watching it fall around your shoulders."

Rica sighed. "I should have remembered, but I was too wrapped up in my own troubles. I'll be a better wife in the future."

"Then I'll die. Because if you get to be a better wife, I'm sure it will kill me," Darryl told her. How could she not see what she already meant to him?

Chapter Nine

GLORIA BROUGHT RICA a note first thing Tuesday morning and, after dropping it off, went back outside without another word. Rica read the note, wondering why Gloria had acted so strangely.

The note promised that Gloria's mother, Mrs. Sternum, would be there as soon as school was out for the day to discuss matters with her. Rica took a deep breath. She wasn't quite prepared for what she wanted to say to the woman, but she'd figure it out as she went.

At lunchtime that day, Darryl surprised her by bringing his lunch to school and eating it with her. He brought a spare chair up to her desk, and the two of them ate together, with many of the children grinning at them.

After he was gone, Rica felt like she had a better idea what she would say to Mrs. Sternum. Somehow the meal with him had made her feel more confident about the entire situation. She herself had waited until many considered her an old maid before marrying. Surely, she could explain the rightness of the action to Gloria's mother.

When she dismissed her students, she waited at her desk, hoping that she would be able to speak clearly of her worries.

Mrs. Sternum walked into the schoolhouse, looking very confident. She sat down in a chair near Rica's desk. "I understand you want to see me."

"Yes, I'm concerned about Gloria. She's such a bright girl, and I think she has a real chance at getting a college scholarship. She needs to stay in school, though, and she needs to keep working on the things that interest her."

Mrs. Sternum shook her head. "My daughter has absolutely no interest in going to college. She's going to get married this weekend."

Rica's jaw dropped. "She is?"

"Yes, her beau asked me for her hand last night. I told her at breakfast this morning that she would marry on Saturday. I do hope you'll come to the wedding, Miss Hughes. I know Gloria thinks a lot of you."

"Mrs. Miller," Rica corrected automatically. She'd been correcting the children about her name for two days, and it just popped out of her mouth. Obviously, the engagement was why Gloria had not spoken that morning. She was upset, and she didn't know what to say. "How does Gloria feel about marrying Mr. Jackson?"

"Oh, she's told you about him? That's wonderful!"

"Actually, it's not. She told me she doesn't like him, and she has no desire to even let him court her. You're condemning your daughter to a lifetime of unhappiness if you force this on her."

Mrs. Sternum frowned. "She's a child. How can she possibly know what she wants?"

"That's my point exactly."

"What's your point?"

Rica smiled. "She's a *child*. A child has no business marrying and taking care of other children. A child should be in school with other children her age, learning everything she can before she's forced to face life as an adult. It isn't the right thing to do to force her to marry at sixteen. I know she's your daughter and not mine, but please at least consider what I'm saying."

"I don't understand her reservations with Mr. Jackson. Does she have a beau here at school? Is that the problem?" Mrs. Sternum genuinely seemed perplexed by her daughter's misgivings.

"No, ma'am. She doesn't have a beau here at school. She's very attentive to her studies. She simply doesn't want to marry a man twice her age and be an instant mother to his six children. She has a right not to want those things." Rica leaned forward, hoping the other woman was listening to her. She needed her to understand that she really would be ruining her daughter's chance to have a future she wanted.

Mrs. Sternum sighed heavily. "I'll talk to her about it. I think she should be grateful I've arranged something like this for her, though. I do it because I care for her, not because I want to ruin her life."

"I do understand that. But your vision for her future is different than hers is. Don't you think a young lady should have a say in her own life?"

Mrs. Sternum got to her feet. "Thank you for your time, Mrs. Miller. I hadn't heard you got married. Best wishes."

"Thank you." Rica watched as the other woman left the building, unsure if what she'd said had made the difference she wanted, but she had tried her very hardest. It's all she'd ever asked from her students, and it was all she could ask of herself.

Instead of going to spend time with her friends, she went straight home and started supper. She had lingered longer than usual, and she didn't want Darryl to have to wait for his meal, though he'd given no indication that he minded waiting. He really was a good husband to her, and she wondered what she'd done to deserve to have a man treat her so well.

She walked to the table and looked at the flowers in the glass there in the middle of the table, and she thought about how sweetly he'd brought them to her. She wasn't a woman who needed riches. She only needed a man who would be thoughtful at the end of his work day. And she'd found the most thoughtful man on the entire West Coast.

Rica was putting supper on the table when the door opened and Darryl walked in. He had another fistful of flowers, but when he set his lunch pail on the counter, he pulled a vase out of it. "I thought it would make you happier if I got you a vase for today's flowers," he said, grinning at her.

She immediately teared up again, taking the flowers and the vase and arranging the flowers fussily. Then she walked into his arms, wrapping hers tightly around him. "You have got to be the most thoughtful man on God's green earth."

"Only on Earth? There are other planets, you know!" He leaned down and buried his face in her hair, which she'd left down. He knew it was for him, and he was thrilled. She thought to accommodate his preferences, and that pleased him more than it probably should.

She laughed. "I haven't been to other planets, but there's a good chance the men there are more considerate than you are. Face the facts, Jack."

He put his wrist against his forehead in a dramatic motion. "Jack? She doesn't even remember my real name!"

Rica stepped toward him, wrapped her arms around his neck, and pulled his head down for her kiss. It was the first time she'd initiated a kiss, and she tried to put all she felt for him into it. When she pulled away, his eyes seemed to be glazed over, and she knew she'd done well. "I'm going to serve supper now. I hope you're hungry!"

He grinned at her, shaking his head. "You are something else, Rica. I'm so glad Gretchen didn't want to marry me."

"She's prettier than I am."

"She's eight months pregnant with someone else's child. I don't need that. I'd have done it for Doris, but I married *you* for me!"

She put supper on the table and sat down across from him, her hand immediately going to his for their prayer. "I talked to Gloria's mother today," she said softly.

"Oh! How did that go?" He'd thought of the situation several times throughout the day, but Rica hadn't mentioned it at lunch.

"I couldn't tell you I was going to at lunch because there were too many children around. She came in right after school and told me that Gloria is getting married on Saturday. She's arranged the marriage."

"Are you serious?"

Rica nodded. "I talked to her about it, telling her about Gloria's hopes and dreams. She told me that Gloria is a child and there's no way she can know what she wants at this time."

"That's right! She's a *child,* so she can't be expected to marry a man with six kids and give up her childhood!"

"My argument exactly. I think she may have listened, but to be honest, I'm just not sure. I hope so. I'll know tomorrow when Gloria comes into school. She didn't even speak to me this morning, just handed me her mother's note and left. I realized why when her mother mentioned she'd told her over breakfast she was expected to marry on Saturday."

He shook his head. "I'll kidnap the girl if I have to. That wedding isn't happening."

Rica grinned. "Thanks for making my problems your own, but I don't think kidnapping one of my students could possibly be the answer."

"Maybe not . . . I could shoot Mr. Jackson!"

"And leave six orphaned children?"

"We'll adopt them all!" He looked around the house with a frown. "No, that's a bad idea. We'd never be able to consummate the marriage if that happened."

Rica couldn't help it. She giggled. And once she started giggling, she simply couldn't stop. After a minute or two with tears streaming down her face and a couple of sips of water to stop the spasm of coughing that went with the giggles, she finally calmed. "You are a breath of fresh air in my life. You make me laugh like no one ever has. How did I live so long without you?"

He tilted his head to one side to think about her question. "Just lucky, I guess."

WHEN GLORIA CAME INTO the schoolhouse the next morning, she had a smile on her face. "Thank you, Mrs. Miller!" She hurried to Rica and hugged her. "My mother said you made her understand that she was doing me a disservice by forcing a marriage. She's going to let me be a child for a while longer."

"That's wonderful!" Rica was thrilled to have her favorite student smiling again.

"And do you know what the best part is?" Gloria asked, her eyes dancing with laughter.

"No, what's the best part?"

"Mr. Jackson came over last night, and she wouldn't even let him see me. She told him I was a child, and I needed to be treated as such. I wouldn't be allowed to court him or even see him until I was old enough to make decisions for myself, and that would be at least a couple of years down the road."

"I'm so happy for you!" Rica couldn't believe her talk with the girl's mother had gone so well, but she was ecstatic. "Now you can live a normal life again. Do you want to sit inside and read until it's time for class to start?" It was something she rarely let any of the students do.

"No, thank you. I think I want to go outside and watch the boys play baseball and maybe talk to some of the other girls. If I have two years of childhood left, I think I should make the most of them instead of running around with my nose in a book all the time." Gloria hurried out the door, a skip to her step that hadn't been there for a while.

Rica smiled as she wrote some sentences to diagram on the board. Everything was right in her world again, and she could concentrate on the dance in two more days. She would finally have a chance to dance with her husband—the man she loved.

BY FRIDAY MORNING, Rica was getting used to sleeping with her husband. It had seemed so strange at first, but now it was second nature. She found herself wrapped in his arms most mornings, and there was nothing she wanted to do about it. Darryl made her feel both loved and protected.

Her friends were both meeting her at the schoolhouse at lunchtime to help her decorate the school for the dance, and she had all of the decorations laid out beside her desk at school.

She practically bounced out of bed to get breakfast started, wanting to start her day as soon as she could. She'd decided that this would be the day when she told Darryl she loved him. While they danced together in her school.

Rica fixed pancakes and bacon for breakfast, wanting to give Darryl a hearty meal before he started his day. With them having the dance that night, she knew it was going to be a very long day for him.

She giggled as she made a pancake into the shape of a heart, but then she was afraid for him to see it, so she put it at the bottom of his stack. Still, she knew she was giving him her heart, even if he didn't.

When she walked over to the bed to wake him, he groaned and pulled her down on top of him. "I need to sleep a little longer. Come back to bed with me."

"You're not a morning person, are you, husband?"

"I would be if mornings came just a little bit later in the day." He held her close, kissing the side of her neck, knowing it would make her squeal. "Who would have thought the schoolteacher would have such a fun side to her?"

"No one. I don't think I had a fun side until I met you," she said, getting to her feet. "Coffee's ready. Come and eat."

"All right." He pulled his pants on while she turned her head, and then he walked to the table, taking a big drink of his coffee. "How do people who don't drink coffee ever get out of bed?"

She shrugged. "I could get up without coffee. I *like* coffee, but I don't need it to kickstart my day."

"Well, I'm not sure I like you then." He grinned at her, and she shook her head.

"You are silly. Sometimes I wonder if I ever laughed before I met you, and now it seems like that's the only thing I ever do."

"I'm glad. If I can bring laughter to your life, then I'm doing something right." He hid a yawn behind his hand. "Do you plan for us to eat before the dance tonight? I only have an hour between work and the dance."

"I think your boss should let you leave early for the dance, but I understand. I'll have something quick ready for you when you get here. Then we'll go over to the school together. I still need to bake some cookies to take with us."

"Sounds good to me. I'll hurry home as quickly as I can. I don't want to get in trouble with the teacher."

"Somehow, I think if you ever do get in trouble with the teacher, you'll be able to talk your way out of it. Teacher has a soft spot for you."

"As she should." Darryl took a bite of his pancakes with a grin on his face. Every day with Rica, he was just a little bit happier than the day before. He didn't know how she did it, but he was married to a very special woman.

Chapter Ten

AT LUNCHTIME, RICA had fun decorating the school with Gretchen and Doris. The three of them worked quickly, along with some of the older girls, to transform the school into a fun place for everyone in the community.

Gloria watched it all with a grin. "I'm going to dance with Charlie tonight. He asked me if he could have a dance already."

Rica smiled at the girl. Charlie was one of the boys she'd be graduating that year, and he was a little more than a year older than Gloria. "I think that sounds like a lot of fun."

"Me too!" Gloria worked to pin a paper chain to one end of the chalkboard. "Do you think any of us will be able to concentrate on our studies this afternoon with the school already decorated for the dance?"

Rica shrugged. "I'm not sure, but if you can't, we won't be able to have a lot more dances."

Gretchen was more excited than anyone. "The first time Reginald kissed me was after a dance in this very school. The last several teachers we've had wouldn't let us use the schoolhouse for dances, so it's been a long time since I've been to one."

Rica realized that Gretchen was much younger than her. She'd only graduated from school in May before Rica started teaching in September. It seemed odd that one of her closest friends had almost been one of her students. She looked over at Gloria and wondered if one day she'd be a friend as well.

Doris had given Pris and Pauline their lunches on one of the school benches, and the little girls watched everything as it happened around them. They were excited because everyone else was happy.

"Who will I dance with?" Pris asked as everyone was decorating.

Doris had an answer for everything. "You can dance with your brothers and with Papa. You might even be able to talk Uncle Darryl into dancing with you. He's a good dancer."

"I have a feeling Uncle Darryl's dances will be taken," Rica said with a smile.

Gretchen grinned over at Rica. "You're really happy. I've seen you smile more in the past hour than I have in all the time I knew you before Darryl arrived here in town. I think marrying him just might be the best thing that ever happened to you."

"I think so, too." Rica couldn't help but grin. "Doris, you sure do have a pretty exceptional twin brother."

"Oh, I know that. He's told me every day of our entire lives!" Doris replied saucily.

Everyone laughed at that. "Are your other brothers like him?" Rica asked, still worried about Gretchen needing to marry someone.

"They're all fun-loving like Darryl, but not all are as conscientious. Twins have a special tie to one another, and if anything upset me, Darryl was there. My other brothers didn't have twin sisters."

"That makes a lot of sense," Rica said. She was glad she finally understood what had made Darryl so understanding.

"Doesn't it? That's my theory. I might not be right, but I will say, anytime I was upset about anything, I'd run to him first. Our other sisters went to each other, but for me it was always Darryl." Doris smiled. "I love watching my twins have that same connection with each other."

Rica loved how Doris had immediately taken on Harv's kids as her own. The moment she'd stepped into town, they'd been hers. It didn't matter to her that she hadn't given birth to them.

Gretchen smiled. "I think we're done. I'll be coming to the dance with the Butlers. Doris is going to need help with her four so she can spend some time dancing in the arms of the man she loves."

Doris smiled. "I don't know what I would have done if I'd come to this town and you two hadn't been here. You've made my life a good one."

"I just hope I bring you half as much joy as you bring me," Gretchen said with tears in her eyes.

They both looked at Rica, so she knew she had to say something. "I'm just glad I can bring joy to your lives."

Doris sighed. "You've been hanging around my brother too much. You're starting to tease everyone."

"You like it, though, right?" Rica asked, a twinkle in her eye.

"I suppose I can tolerate it." Doris took the girls by the hands and led them toward the door. "See you tonight, sister!"

If the pupils were inattentive that afternoon, Rica didn't notice. She was too antsy for the dance herself. She dismissed school fifteen minutes early so she could go home and start supper. She wanted to be able to leave for the dance just as soon as Darryl had eaten. No one would be able to get into the school until she was there to unlock it.

She started supper, and she went to her wardrobe and picked out a pretty purple dress that she had never worn before. It had been made for a dance that she'd just known a young man back home would ask her to, and he'd asked someone else instead.

Now she had a reason to wear it, and she couldn't be more excited. She laid it out on the bed to air out, planning to put it on right before Darryl was due home. She spent some time on her hair, trying a new hairstyle that swept up a lot of her hair but left some of her curls hanging loosely around her face. She knew it would please Darryl, but she wanted to make sure she looked like a schoolteacher as well.

She put supper on the table and hurried to change before he came in, smoothing the skirt of her dress down and looking into her little hand mirror. She couldn't see the full effect of the dress, but she hoped it looked as good as she thought it did.

Darryl came in as she set the mirror down, and he stopped in the doorway. His face and hands were dirty from his hard day at work, so he went to the sink and pumped the water, cleaning himself up. "I'm afraid I'll muss you too much if I touch you."

She laughed. "I can be fixed. As long as you don't get my dress dirty, I won't mind even a little bit."

He walked to her and cupped her face in his hands, his lips descending on hers. "Do you have any idea what it means to me to have you waiting for me at the end of a hard day of work? I'm not complaining about what I do, but you make everything worthwhile."

Rica smiled at that. "Gretchen commented today how much more I smile now that you're in my life. I don't think I can express the difference in me since your arrival."

"Well, I think we should stop this mutual admiration and eat our supper. Someone has to be to the school in a few minutes." Darryl grinned at her, sitting down at the table where his supper waited for him.

"As soon as I've eaten, I'm going to put the dishes to soak in the sink and head over to the school. You're going to need to change and follow me over."

He nodded. "I can do that. I was hoping you wouldn't mind going over on your own for just a little while."

She shrugged. "I'm used to being a wallflower at dances, remember?"

"I do remember. I'm used to running around begging every girl there to dance with me and hoping one of them will have pity on me!"

Rica grinned. "Somehow I have a very hard time believing that. You don't seem like the type of man who has ever lacked for female attention."

"You just don't know how bad our reputations were back home. Even ask Doris. No one would look at any of us romantically."

"So none of your other siblings are married?"

"Mary got married, but no one is quite sure how. Elizabeth married a man who worked for her. Susan was a mail order bride. Wally was a mail order groom. Do you see a recurring theme here?"

"Well, I wouldn't have been able to resist you, even with your reputation. I would have taken one look into those big brown eyes, and I'd have fallen at your feet."

"That sounds like something I would really enjoy! It's too bad you weren't there to put me out of my misery sooner." He winked at her. "Actually, I think that if I'd met you sooner, I wouldn't have been ready for you. I needed to go through life just as long as I did, so I'd appreciate you like I should." He took her hand and brought it to his lips. "I'm ready to dance all night with you."

As soon as they finished eating, she soaked the dishes. "I'm heading over. Please hurry!" Rica told him.

"I will. You get everything opened up, and don't dance with any other dashing men who come your way."

She laughed. "As if I would!" She hurried out the door to the school, opening the building at ten minutes before seven. As soon as it was open, women brought in cookies and cakes, and the small band set up on the teacher's platform.

The turnout was bigger than she'd expected. Some people would have to dance outside, and she loved the idea of being one of them. Dancing under the stars with the man she loved sounded like one of the most romantic things she could possibly do.

By the time Darryl joined her, they were on the second song. People all over were dancing and enjoying themselves. She even spotted Gloria dancing with her young man.

Darryl walked to her and bowed low. "Mrs. Miller, may I have the pleasure of this dance?"

Rica smiled and nodded, going right into his arms. There was nowhere else in the world she would rather be than right there with the man she loved. The schoolhouse was crowded, so she suggested dancing outside under the stars as she'd thought about just a short while before.

As soon as they were away from others, she met his gaze with her own. It was dark, but some people had hung lanterns up around the playground. "Darryl, there's something I've been meaning to tell you."

"There is? What's that?" He seemed so at ease and so happy with her there, dancing in the moonlight.

"I thought this would be a good place to tell you that you've changed my life. The things that were mundane before all have meaning now. I love you with everything inside me, Darryl Miller."

His grin was so big, she was glad she told him, even if he never reciprocated her feelings. "I knew I was done for the minute I saw you. I was so glad to find out I wasn't marrying Gretchen. I love you right back, Frederica!"

"You do? Really?"

"Really. There's no one on this planet who would be a better wife for me." He leaned down and kissed her softly.

Rica should have protested that he was kissing her in front of her students, but she just couldn't make herself care about it. "Thank you for coming into my life."

"Does this mean the courtship part of our marriage is over?" he asked with a grin.

"I hope the courtship part of our marriage never ends. But it does mean we can move on to other things as well as courtship."

"Do you think your students would notice if I swept you up in my arms and carried you off to our house?" He glanced over at the house and thought about how far it really was.

She laughed. "Yes, I do. Dance is over at nine. You can wait that long."

"I've already waited a lifetime for you. What's another couple of hours?"

KIRSTEN OSBOURNE IS an extremely prolific writer who lives in Idaho with her husband of twenty years, her son, and a hyperactive dog. She loves to bring joy to her readers by giving each couple she writes about a happily ever after.